CHASING A STAR

OTHER BOOKS BY
NORMA CHARLES

Bank Job [with James Heneghan], Orca, 2009

The Girl in the Backseat, Ronsdale, 2008

Boxcar Kid, Dundurn, 2007

Sophie's Friend in Need, Dundurn, 2004

All the Way to Mexico, Raincoast, 2003

Fuzzy Wuzzy, Coteau, 2002

Criss Cross, Double Cross, Dundurn, 2002

The Accomplice, Raincoast, 2001

Sophie, Sea to Sea, Dundurn, 1999

Runaway, Coteau, 1999

Dolphin Alert! Nelson, 1998

Darlene's Shadow, General, 1991

A Bientôt, Croco, Scholastic, 1991

See You Later, Alligator, Scholastic, 1991

April Fool Heroes, Nelson, 1989

Un Poney Embarrassant, Les Edition Heritage, 1989

No Place for a Horse, General, 1988

Amanda Grows Up, Scholastic, 1978

CHASING
a Star

NORMA CHARLES

RONSDALE PRESS

RONSDALE PRESS
3350 West 21st Avenue, Vancouver, B.C., Canada V6S 1G7
www.ronsdalepress.com

Typesetting: Julie Cochrane, in Minion 12 pt on 16
Cover Photography: Julie Cochrane
Cover Design: Julie Cochrane
Paper: Ancient Forest Friendly "Silva" (FSC) — 100% post-consumer waste, totally chlorine-free and acid-free

Ronsdale Press wishes to thank the following for their support of its publishing program: the Canada Council for the Arts, the Government of Canada through the Book Publishing Industry Development Program (BPIDP), the British Columbia Arts Council, and the Province of British Columbia through the British Columbia Book Publishing Tax Credit program.

Library and Archives Canada Cataloguing in Publication

Charles, Norma M.
    Chasing a star / Norma Charles.

ISBN 978-1-55380-077-4

    1. Scott, Barbara Ann, 1928– — Juvenile fiction.
I. Title.

PS8555.H4224C43 2009   jC813'.54   C2009-902164-1

At Ronsdale Press we are committed to protecting the environment. To this end we are working with Markets Initiative (www.oldgrowthfree.com) and printers to phase out our use of paper produced from ancient forests. This book is one step towards that goal.

Printed in Canada by Marquis Printing, Quebec

for Trevor,
always a star in my eyes

ACKNOWLEDGEMENTS

I would like to thank my fellow writers who gave me invaluable suggestions and advice for this book, especially James Heneghan, Linda Bailey and Beryl Young. I would also like to thank my brother Ron Finnigan, motorcycle guru, and my aunt Rita Lacerte for sharing her wonderful autograph books from the 1940s with me. As well, I'd like to thank Barbara Ann Scott for inspiring countless young skaters with her perseverance and dedication to excellence.

1
Sophie LaGrange,
Skating Star

AUGUST 31, 1951, was the day Sophie LaGrange's life changed forever.

The radio was tuned to CKNW, the local station, and Doris Day was singing *"Zippa dee doo dah, Zippa dee ay. My, oh my, what a wonderful day . . ."*

Sophie was imagining her roller skates were ice skates and the basement was a gigantic arena. Sunlight filtered through the dusty windows set high in the basement walls. She zigzagged around the three wooden posts in the centre of the dim room. Her roller skate key swung back and forth from a string around her neck.

"I'm a famous figure skating star," she whispered to herself. As famous as the Olympic gold medal winner, Barbara Ann Scott, and she was on the ice at the Olympics, gliding to organ music blaring out over loudspeakers. She was wearing a golden star cape like that of her favourite comic book hero, Star Girl. The cape unfurled and fluttered behind her, and the smooth concrete floor was ice, glass-smooth ice.

The bleachers were filled with an excited crowd, shouting and cheering *Bravo, Barbara Ann!* They were cheering *Bravo! Bravo!* They'd never seen such grace. Such crossovers. Such turns. Such talent. She was a blur of motion.

Sophie raised her hand to acknowledge the cheering crowd. She blew the people kisses and smiled her best smile, dazzling them.

In breathless admiration, the crowd rose to its feet.

She bowed her head and started her spins. She twirled around and around, her star cape swirling about her. The crowd exploded with excitement. She was the star! The star of the Olympics! The Ice Skating World Champion. Her wonderful performance would earn her another gold medal for Canada. Her name would go down in history. The whole country would be overcome with pride.

There was a noisy commotion from upstairs, loud voices and thumping on the basement ceiling, but Sophie ignored it. She was having way too much fun skating around in her imaginary world.

She clamped her hands behind her back and took long

smooth strides. Faster and faster she flew. As she streaked past the furnace with its heating-duct arms snaking along the ceiling, the noise from upstairs grew louder.

Sophie shut her eyes to close out the sound. Bam! She crashed, head-first into a thick post. She bounced backwards and landed on her backside with a thump.

"Sophie! Sophie! The aunties are here!" Her little brother Zephram rushed down the stairs. "The aunties are here!"

"What?" Sophie rubbed her throbbing forehead. "What did you say?" It was a toss-up what hurt more, her head or her backside.

"What are you doing sitting on the floor?" Zephram asked.

"Just . . . um . . . resting," she told him.

Her brother's eyes were huge with excitement. "Papa's back from the train station with the aunties. They're finally here!"

Sophie undid the straps and kicked off her roller skates. Then she raced him up the stairs.

Doris Day sang on the radio, *"Wonderful feeling! Wonderful day!"*

2

The Aunties Are Here!

SOPHIE AND HER little brother tumbled into the living room.

Valises and boxes were everywhere, surrounding two beautiful women who looked familiar. They were jolly and oh, so glamorous, in their high-heeled shoes and their fancy hats, glossy red lipstick and nail polish. And perfume. Sophie inhaled. They made the living room smell like a flower garden.

The aunties had arrived by train, all the way from Montreal.

"Now who's this?" The taller auntie stared at Sophie's little brother. The auntie was wearing a blue jacket and a long matching skirt with a slit that ran all the way up the side and she had a mound of curls piled on her head. "It can't be Zephram."

"But it is," Maman said, smiling at him.

"He was just a baby when we saw him last. Now look at him! He's all grown up. Come here and give your Auntie Claudine a big kiss, *mon petit chou-chou*." She embraced Zephram, kissing him until he giggled.

"Now my turn," the other auntie said. She was shorter, but just as glamorous, with a shiny brown dress the exact shade of her shiny brown hair. Auntie Marie-Rose.

Four-year-old Zephram was passed from one aunt to the other like a giggling teddy bear, to be hugged and kissed. He was loving every minute of all the attention.

Auntie Claudine turned to Sophie. "And this lovely young lady? Who's she? Not our little Sophie? No! Impossible for someone to change so much in just a year."

"It's been more than two years since we moved to the west coast," Papa said, bringing in another load of boxes and valises.

"Two years? *Mais non!* I remember when you left. It's like yesterday. Come and give your auntie a big hug too, my beauty." She enveloped Sophie in a perfumed cloud. "You must have the boys all lining up, clamouring for dates."

Sophie blushed. Suddenly, she felt tongue-tied and shy, which was crazy because she'd known Auntie Claudine, her mother's youngest sister, and Auntie Marie-Rose, their cousin, forever. They'd been regular visitors at their home in Montreal. She just didn't remember them being so very glamorous. She really liked Auntie Claudine, but Auntie Marie-Rose had always been her favourite.

"Look at you!" Maman stared at Auntie Marie-Rose as she took her coat. "You're so thin. Thin as a shadow."

"Not at all," Auntie Marie Rose said, smoothing out her skirt.

"You must be working much too hard at that new job. We'll have to see what we can do to fatten you up with some good home cooking."

Sophie noticed her older brother Arthur, who was thirteen, lurking uncomfortably around the living room door. She could tell he was feeling as shy as she was.

He couldn't hide though. Auntie Claudine grabbed him and pressed him to her bosom in a big hug. His face flushed as she passed him on to Auntie Marie-Rose who also hugged him, laughing at his red cheeks and ruffling his dark hair.

"Now where are the big boys?" Auntie Claudine asked. "Joseph and Henri? I bet they've grown to be so handsome too."

"Both at work," Papa said. "Joseph has a summer job at the mill. And Henri, he's working at Young's Market."

"I can't believe it! That must mean they're both all grown up."

"Too grown up." Maman shook her head. "Wait until you see them. Joseph has to shave every day. They'll be home soon for supper."

"Well, we have gifts for everyone." Auntie Claudine flipped her big valise open, and delved into the contents. "Should we wait until the big brothers come home, or do you want yours now?"

"Now," Zephram squealed. "Oh, now, please."

"All right, here you are, *mon petit chou*." She pulled out a miniature hockey stick and puck. "Now let me tell you. This is no ordinary hockey stick."

"Wow!" Arthur said, forgetting about being shy. "It's signed by Maurice Richard. The 'Rocket'. You lucky guy, Zeph!"

"So you're a Rocket Richard fan too?" Auntie Claudine asked him.

"Who isn't? He's the fastest man on skates that ever lived."

"Good," Auntie Marie-Rose said. "Because we brought this for you." Out of her valise she pulled a package and shook it out. It was a red and blue hockey sweater with a big number 9 on the back.

Arthur's eyes popped. "Wow! A Montreal Canadien hockey sweater, with the Rocket's number!" He grinned and held it in front of his chest. The sweater was enormous, reaching down to his knees. "It's perfect. Thank you."

Sophie's stomach fluttered with excitement. It felt like Christmas morning, she thought, as she sat on the piano bench beside Auntie Marie-Rose and smiled at her. When her aunt smiled back, Sophie saw dark shadows under her eyes she'd never noticed before.

"From *mon oncle* Gerard's farm, the best maple syrup in all Quebec." Auntie Claudine presented a large jug to Maman.

"How lovely!" Maman said. "Papa's favourite. I'll make some crêpes to have with it tomorrow. You know we can't get the real maple syrup here on the coast."

"And for *La Belle*," Auntie Claudine turned to Sophie. "Something very, very special," she sang.

"Yes," Auntie Marie-Rose said, pulling out a rectangular box tied with a red ribbon. "I carried your gift on my lap all the way from Ottawa so it wouldn't get damaged. Now, I hope you still like dolls, *chérie*."

"Dolls?" Sophie croaked, her heart sinking. She hadn't played with dolls for ages. What twelve-year-old did? Even before they'd left Montreal, she'd outgrown them. Didn't the aunties know she wasn't a little kid any more? It had been years since she'd even looked at a doll, much less played with one. She was so disappointed she could barely mutter, "*Merci.*"

Before Auntie Marie-Rose could give the box to Sophie, the roar of a motor blasted through the front windows.

"My goodness!" Maman exclaimed, her hand over her heart. "What in the world is that?"

"*Sacré bleu!*" Papa said, checking out the front window.

Thankful for the distraction, Sophie rushed to pull open the front door. Clouds of smoky exhaust drifted into the house.

"It's Joseph," she shouted, coughing. "And Henri. And they're on a motorcycle!"

Sophie's two oldest brothers were home.

3

The Bikers

SOPHIE'S OLDEST BROTHER Joseph, who was eighteen, was revving up the motorcycle beside the gate. Henri, her second oldest brother, sixteen, was sitting behind Joseph. He climbed off the motorcycle, grinning.

The family poured out of the house.

Zephram scrambled down the steps past Sophie. "Wow! A motorcycle!" he cried out. "Can I have a ride, Joe? Can you give me a ride?"

Maman stayed up on the porch. "Wherever did that dangerous machine come from, Joseph?" she called down, annoyance in her voice. "What are you doing with it?"

Joseph pulled off his goggles and helmet, and grinned at her. "It's mine, Maman. All mine. I bought it with my last paycheque from the mill. The owner threw in the leather jacket and this flying helmet and goggles. Pretty good, eh? I gave Henri a ride home from work."

Joseph's grin was infectious. Sophie found herself grinning back and jumping around the shiny blue motorcycle with Zephram.

"So now, who wants a ride around the block?" Joseph asked.

"Me, me!" Zephram shouted, shoving Sophie out of the way.

"Just a minute, boys," Maman said. "Come and say hello to your aunties."

Auntie Claudine whistled. "Look at you two! Must be this west coast air that makes everyone grow so tall and handsome."

"Now little Joseph even has his own motorcycle!" Auntie Marie-Rose said, hugging him. "Fancy that!"

Sophie noticed that "little" Joseph was now a head taller than her aunt.

Joseph lifted Auntie Marie-Rose and twirled her around.

"Put me down!" she squealed. "Put me down!"

He laughed and set her down beside his new bike.

Papa was examining the bike, shaking his head. "I'm not sure a motorcycle is such a good idea, Son. They're dangerous machines."

"But I'm a careful driver. You said so when you taught me to drive the car."

"A car is one thing. But a Norton with a 500 cc motor?" Papa shook his head. "We'll have to talk about it."

Zephram pushed Sophie out of the way again and wriggled between Papa and Joseph, climbing onto the seat. He gripped the handlebars and the motor roared, belching out grey smoke.

Sophie leaped back, her heart pounding.

"Turn off that motor!" Papa shouted, snatching Zephram.

Joseph turned it off. All was quiet for a moment.

Maman cleared her throat and scolded, trying to wave the smoke away. "*Eh, mon Dieu!* Joseph will get into some terrible accident on that dangerous thing. I know he will. I just know it!"

Joseph said. "I think you should have the first ride, Maman, and you'll see how carefully I drive and how very safe it is."

But Maman said no. She had to go back to the kitchen to see to supper. And she needed Papa's help to put the extra leaf in the kitchen table.

"We'll talk about the motorcycle later," Papa said as he followed Maman inside.

Joseph rolled his eyes. Sophie could tell he was annoyed.

"So can I have a ride now, Joe?" she asked.

"Our company all the way from Quebec should get the first ride," he said, smiling at Auntie Claudine.

"Great! I'll love to go first," she said, leaning on Sophie's shoulder as she climbed onto the back seat behind Joseph. "Where do I put my feet?" she asked.

"There are some pegs here." Sophie showed her aunt where she could rest her high-heeled shoes on the pegs on either side of the back wheel. The slit in her tight skirt gaped open all the way up her leg, revealing the top of her stocking and her garter.

"Oo-la-la!" Auntie Marie-Rose laughed and covered Arthur's gawking eyes with her hand.

Auntie Claudine screeched when Joseph took off, spraying up gravel.

They were back soon.

"What a ball!" Auntie Claudine exclaimed, climbing off the bike. Her cheeks were red with excitement. "You must try it, Marie-Rose."

Auntie Marie-Rose wasn't so enthusiastic. She bit her lip as she sat "side-saddle," balancing on the back seat with her ankles crossed demurely. When the motorcycle took off, she shrieked as she swayed precariously.

"Hang on!" Sophie and Auntie Claudine shouted. "Hang on!"

She gripped Joseph's waist with one hand and the back of the seat with the other but the breeze whipped up her full skirt into a parachute and they could see her lacy pink petticoats.

Arthur grinned at Sophie and bounced his lacrosse ball to her.

"You shouldn't stare like that, you know," she told him as she caught the ball and bounced it back to him. "It's not polite."

He shrugged and, still grinning, tossed the ball back to her. He was wearing his new "Rocket-Richard" hockey sweater. It flopped around his knees, and the long sleeves covered his hands.

After Zephram, it was finally Sophie's turn for a ride. She was glad she was wearing Arthur's hand-me-down jeans so she didn't have to worry about her skirt flying all over the place. She straddled the motorcycle's backseat, found the pegs with her feet, and clung to Joseph's waist. She leaned her cheek against his smooth leather jacket, smelling it. Nice.

Joseph revved up the motor and they took off, spewing out gravel and dust. Sophie crouched behind her brother's back, but still the wind sucked away her breath and made her eyes water. She shut her mouth to keep out the dust, and crouched lower. The vibrations from the motor made her whole body shake and tremble. When they came to the end of the block, she had to lean into the corner as they turned and her knee almost touched the gravel road. Scary.

There was her friend Elizabeth in her front yard, playing with her dog Bunny. Elizabeth ran to the road. "Sophie!" she called out. "Hey, Sophie!"

The dog barked at them.

But Sophie didn't dare let go of Joseph's waist to wave back. She just nodded and held on tight as they sped by.

As they rounded the next corner, two other motorcycles blasted out from the side-street. They cut Joseph and Sophie off, forcing them off the road.

Sophie's heart lurched. She gripped Joseph's waist as his motorcycle plunged into the long grass. The motor died and the bike jolted to a stand-still.

The two motorcycles spun around and headed straight back at them.

"Watch out!" Joseph shouted and flung out his arm to protect Sophie.

She squealed and ducked behind his back.

At the last very moment, the motorcycles veered away. They were big black motorcycles and both riders were wearing dark goggles and army officer's hats with shiny black visors.

Sophie forgot about being shy with strangers. She popped up and yelled, "How dare you scare us like that!" She shook her fist at the bikers. "How dare you!"

The lead motorcycle driver wheeled back and screeched to a stop beside them. He stared down at them and then he started laughing, flashing white teeth.

That made Sophie even madder. "You big gorilla," she yelled in his face. "You ran us off the road on purpose."

"Quite a little whipper-snapper, you got there," the biker said to Joseph and laughed some more. The other biker started laughing at her as well.

A car pulled up behind the motorcycles. A man around

Papa's age peered out the side window. "Everything all right there? Anyone need a hand?"

The bikers stopped laughing. There was a short silence. Then Joseph said, "We're okay, sir. Thanks for stopping."

The man nodded and the car left slowly.

Sophie stared back at both bikers, narrowing her eyes. But she held her tongue.

The lead biker was big with broad shoulders and black hair that flopped down over his eyebrows. He was chewing gum. "Bit of advice, kid," he growled at her. "You want to watch that temper. Might get you into big trouble one day." Then he nodded at Joseph, gunned his motor and his motorcycle took off up the hill. The other motorcyclist took off after him, peppering Joseph and Sophie with gravel.

The bikers both raised gloved fists. Two words were hammered out with nail studs on the backs of their black jackets: Satan's Rebels.

"What's that all about?" Sophie asked her brother, blinking hard. Her eyes smarted from the dust and her heart was hammering.

"Don't really know," Joseph muttered. He started up the motor again and steered his bike back onto the road. Soon they roared up to the front gate of their house.

When Joseph turned off the motor, Sophie wanted to ask him more about the bikers, but Maman was on the front porch looking worried.

"There you are, you two." She waved a dish towel at them.

"Supper's ready. Come and wash up."

"Okay, we'll be right there." Joseph parked the motorcycle near the front hedge.

Sophie climbed off. Her legs were trembling. "That's the most exciting ride I've ever had in my life," she said, rubbing her knees. "Even more exciting than the giant roller coaster at the PNE. I thought those bikers were going to plow right into us."

"Not a chance." Joseph pulled off the aviator helmet and goggles. "They were just fooling around."

"That 'Satan's Rebels' on their jackets. I haven't seen that before."

"It's the name of a motorcycle gang. I heard they're moving up here from down south. I don't think they appreciated you telling them off like that," he laughed. "Better not mention them to Mom. Or Dad either. You know how they worry."

"Sure do." Sophie smiled up at him.

"Anyway, I'm glad you liked the ride, shortie," he said, tousling her hair, and led the way into the house.

4

Why So Glum, Chum?

AS SOPHIE FOLLOWED her brother through the living room, she barely glanced at the stupid doll box her aunties had brought for her. She felt like stomping on it, but instead she just nudged it with her toe on her way to the bathroom to wash her hands and try to smooth down her unruly curly hair. Maman had given her a short haircut at the beginning of the summer, but it had grown back to its usual length, down to almost her shoulders.

As Sophie joined everyone else around the big wooden table in the kitchen she was thinking that maybe if she ignored the doll box, it would somehow magically disappear.

She took a deep sniff of tonight's supper. Yum! Maman had made a special meal for the aunties. Roasted chicken with potatoes and carrots, and homemade buns and a big salad of lettuce and tomatoes from Papa's garden and, for dessert, a couple of enormous fresh peach pies.

In spite of the delicious smells, Sophie's insides were a pit of turmoil. The excitement of the motorcycle ride tussled with that knot of disappointment about the silly doll her aunties had brought for her.

She squeezed onto the end of the bench along the wall beside her little brother and crossed her arms over her fluttering stomach.

"Eat up, everyone, before it gets cold," Maman urged. "Henri, pass the chicken to Marie-Rose. We must try to fatten her up a little, now."

It turned out to be such a jolly supper that Sophie soon forgot her worries and dug into the delicious meal with everyone else. There was lots of talk and laughter about the old days in Montreal when the LaGrange family used to live there, and gossip about how the other relatives were getting along, who had new babies and who was engaged and married and who'd died.

After everyone had finished the main course, scraping the serving bowls and dishes clean, Maman got up to put water on the stove for tea.

Sophie helped her collect the plates since it was her turn to clear the table that night.

"The ice cream," Maman said. "Henri, did you remember

to bring the ice cream to have with our peach pie?"

"Oh, no! I completely forgot. When Joseph arrived with his new motorcycle, I rushed out of the store to get a ride home. Sorry, Maman."

"I'll get it now," Joseph said, getting up from his chair. "Let's go, Henri. I bet we're back before that kettle has even boiled for the tea."

The roar of Joseph's motorcycle blasted in through the windows and Maman's brow creased with worry. "Those machines are so dangerous," she said, shaking her head.

"That's true," Papa said. "We'll have to talk with Joseph about keeping it."

"You don't think he'd join one of those nasty motorcycle gangs you hear about, do you?" Maman said.

"Let's hope our Joseph has more sense than that," Papa said.

Sophie wondered if the Satan's Rebels gang members were lying in wait for her brother. She guessed they weren't because he and Henri were back with the brick of ice cream even before the kettle had boiled for tea. Joseph had been right about that.

The peach pie with ice cream was extra delicious. In spite of the fluttery knots in her stomach, Sophie swallowed the last heavenly morsel from her plate.

"You haven't lost your touch with pastry, Alma," Auntie Claudine said, licking the last crumbs from her fork. "Your pies were always the very best."

"That's what I keep telling her," Papa said. "She should

enter her pies in competition at the PNE. She'd win first prize, for sure."

"Oh, you two. You just want a second piece. Here you are," Maman said, putting extra pieces into Claudine and Papa's plates. "Anyone else for another piece?"

Sophie was too stuffed for more dessert so she shook her head.

After everyone had finished eating, Maman said, "If you've all had enough, let's go into the living room. I want to hear all about cousin Matilde and those new twin babies of hers. How's she ever managing?"

"But what about the dishes?" Auntie Marie-Rose asked.

"The kids will take care of them," Maman said, leading the way to the living room.

Sophie wasn't in any rush to join them. She'd have to open that doll box and pretend to be thrilled about getting a stupid new doll. She dawdled clearing the table, stacking the plates and cups into piles.

"What's taking so long, Sophie?" Arthur complained. He was standing at a sink full of sudsy water, but no dishes to wash. "We haven't got all day, you know."

"Yeah, get the lead out, Soph." Henri flicked his dish towel at her.

"Okay, okay," Sophie muttered. She carried over the rest of the cups and plates and dumped them into the sudsy water.

"Why so glum, chum?" Henri asked her as he polished his eye-glasses with his dish towel.

"Nothing's wrong."

"I bet I know what's eating her," Arthur said. "She can't wait to get back into the living room and play with her brand new cute little dolly. Right, Soph?"

"Yeah, right," Sophie said. "How old do the aunties think I am, anyway? Six maybe? Don't they know I'm twelve now, and about to start high school? You know anyone who still plays with dolls in high school?"

"Dolly, dolly, dolly," Arthur teased, blowing soap bubbles at her.

She grabbed the broom to bash him one on the head.

But Henri pushed between them. "Grow up, you two," he said, glowering down at them both.

"He started it," Sophie grumbled. She turned her back on her brothers and swept the floor, taking her time to get all the crumbs from under the benches. But she couldn't delay any longer. There was no way of avoiding it. She may as well face the music. She got her best fake smile ready and clomped into the living room.

"Ah, Sophie," Auntie Marie-Rose said. "There you are. Now you can open your present."

"My present? Oh, um, yes. I almost forgot," she mumbled. She picked up the silly doll box gingerly, untied the ribbon and lifted the lid.

"Oh my!" she gasped. "It, it's a Barbara Ann Scott figure skating doll!" She couldn't believe it. From a bed of tissue paper, a doll with long blond ringlets and shiny blue eyes that opened and closed, stared up at her. Her pink lips were curled into a smile and Sophie spotted a row of tiny white teeth. The doll was wearing a sparkly blue dress with a short skirt trimmed with soft white rabbit fur and on her feet was a pair of tiny, but perfectly shaped, leather ice skates with genuine metal blades.

"She's beautiful," Sophie said, grinning. "Just beautiful. Thank you! Thanks a lot!"

"Look," Auntie Marie-Rose said. "There's something else in there that you'll like, I bet."

Sophie searched around in the crinkly tissue paper and came upon a tiny red box.

"Open it, open it," Auntie Marie-Rose said, clapping her hands.

Inside the box was a perfect pair of roller skates, white leather, like the ice skates, but with four tiny wheels instead of blades. This doll wasn't an ordinary baby doll at all. She was a girl doll. A famous girl doll who could roller skate as well as ice skate.

Sophie's heart was beating fast, doing a loop-da-loop in her chest. She gently lifted the doll out of her crinkly tissue paper bed and hugged her.

"Oh, *merci*, thank you. Thank you very much," she said to her aunties. "I just love Barbara Ann Scott. I've wanted one of these dolls forever." She didn't have to use a fake smile after all. The smile she gave them was as genuine as the doll's leather skates.

"We know." Auntie Marie-Rose hugged her. "Your mother told us."

"Barbara Ann Scott is our Canadian hero," Auntie Claudine said. "She won the gold medal for Canada for figure skating a few years ago. The only gold medal Canada has ever won in the Winter Olympics."

"Except for hockey," Papa said.

"Right. Except for hockey."

"And next February, at the Winter Olympics in Norway, I bet we take home another gold medal for hockey like we did last time," Papa said.

"What about Barbara Ann Scott?" Sophie asked. "Won't she win us another Olympic gold medal for figure skating?"

"No, she's skating professionally now," Auntie Claudine said. "When you turn professional, you can't compete in the Olympics anymore. She's the star in a show from Hollywood. The Hollywood Ice Review, I think it's called. Touring all across the country. That's what I heard, anyway."

"I knew her in high school in Ottawa," Auntie Marie-Rose said. "She had no time for anything except skating. I remember her saying she had to practise at the Minto Skating Club at least six hours a day, every single day, even Sundays."

"You actually met her?" Sophie asked. "You actually met Barbara Ann Scott?"

"Hundreds of times. Every day, in fact." Auntie Marie-Rose nodded. "We were in the same class in grade twelve for math and chemistry."

"Is she as pretty as her photos in the newspapers?" Maman asked.

"Even prettier," Auntie Marie-Rose said.

"All her hard work practising certainly paid off," Papa said. "That's a good lesson for you kids. To achieve something worthwhile, you must be ready to work hard for it."

"Now it's time to get your baggage into the bedroom." Maman clapped her hands. "You can have Sophie's room," she said to the aunties. "She'll sleep on the sofa here in the living room."

Oh no! She was supposed to have cleaned up her room for the guests. Sophie dashed from the living room and plowed through her clothes and books on the floor in her bedroom. She scooped them up and stuffed them all into the closet. She had to lean hard on the door to get it closed.

"This is a great room," Auntie Marie-Rose said from the doorway. "Thanks for letting us use it."

"You're welcome." Sophie patted the bedspread smooth. "Just don't open the closet door, okay?"

"Don't worry. We won't. We'll use these hooks behind the door to hang up our clothes."

Sophie skipped back into the living room and put her beautiful new doll on top of the piano, propping her against the wall. She smoothed back her pretty blond curls under the tiara and fluffed up the sparkly skirt.

Wouldn't it be wonderful if one day she could actually meet such a star in real life? Meeting the famous Barbara Ann Scott. That would be a dream come true.

5

Shopping with the Aunties

THE NEXT DAY WAS Saturday. The last weekend before school started.

"I thought we girls could go shopping downtown in New West this morning," Maman said to the aunties as they finished their crêpes, rolled in the delicious maple syrup from Quebec. "Papa doesn't need the car for work today, so we can use it. I want to go to Eaton's to buy Sophie her uniform for the new school."

"I'd love to come," Auntie Claudine said.

"A shopping spree! I wouldn't miss it for the world," Auntie Marie-Rose said, smiling at Sophie.

Although she didn't feel very happy, Sophie smiled back.

She ached to get back to the basement to practise roller skating and pretend she was an Olympic star, like Barbara Ann Scott. But that would have to wait until they returned. She knew Maman wouldn't let her get out of shopping, especially since they were going mainly to buy her clothes for her new school.

New school. She hated thinking about that. When she did, her insides went all topsy-turvy. She wouldn't know one single other girl at the new school. Everyone from her grade six class last term was going to Como Lake High School. She'd wanted to go there too, but Maman had declared she'd heard Como Lake High was a very rough school. So she had arranged to send her only daughter to St. Ann's Academy, an all-girls school in New Westminster where the nuns would do a very good job teaching her, she said.

"But it's too far to walk all the way to New Westminster," Auntie Marie-Rose said. "How will Sophie get to school every day?"

"There's a bus at the bottom of Blue Mountain Road on Brunette. It will take her right into town. We'll drive by the bus stop for her school today."

"Can I go shopping too?" Zephram asked.

"Come and play baseball at the park with Arthur and me," Papa said. "Lots more fun than traipsing after those ladies."

"Goody!" Zephram said. "I'll get my ball."

Papa was sipping coffee and reading the newspaper. "Listen to this," he said. "'Bikers Battle Over Territory. In recent months a notorious motorcycle gang from south of the border has infiltrated the Vancouver region in a search for new recruits. Police suspect this gang, known as Satan's Rebels, of being involved in illegal activities such as robbery, extortion and even kidnapping.' Sounds like a bad bunch of hooligans. Good thing we don't live in Vancouver."

"Oh dear," Maman said, "I hope they don't come out here and start causing trouble."

Sophie gasped. Satan's Rebels! Illegal activities! Kidnapping! She was about to tell Papa that she and Joseph had actually met a couple of the bikers, but she remembered she'd promised Joseph she wouldn't say anything about them. She squeezed her lips shut tight.

"Aren't you coming, Sophie?" Maman said. "We're leaving soon. You better get ready."

Sophie nodded as she carried her plate to the sink. She didn't dare say anything to Maman either. She knew her parents were still not happy about Joseph's new motorcycle. Especially Maman. They had decided that he could keep his motorcycle for the time being, but they'd be sure to change their minds if they heard about the encounter with those rough Satan's Rebels gang members.

Sophie sat in the backseat of Papa's blue Mercury with Auntie Marie-Rose. Her aunt smiled at her as she filed her long red fingernails. Sophie thought even when she smiled, she still had that sad look in her eyes. She couldn't think of how to ask her about it. She pushed her own hands into her pockets because her nails were ragged and even a little dirty from digging around her tomato plants in Papa's garden. Some of the tomatoes were already ripe and they'd had plenty of salads with his lettuce, prickly cucumbers, radishes and green onions.

Maman drove along the road beside the river. As they went under the span of the Pattullo Bridge she slowed the car down.

"That's the bus stop where you'll get off the bus next week, Sophie." She pointed to the side of the road. "Then you just walk up the hill to the new school. Do you see it? It's that grey building up there."

Sophie stared out at a big grey stone building that stood at the top of a grassy slope surrounded by trees. Again, her insides fluttered with dread.

"It'll be fine." Auntie Marie-Rose patted her arm. "You'll see."

They were soon right downtown in New Westminster. Maman parked the car across the street from Eaton's.

"My! What a grand street!" Auntie Claudine said, gathering her purse and climbing out of the car. "Look at all those shops."

"This is Columbia Street," Maman said. "You should see Royal Avenue, up the hill. Now, that's really grand. They call it Royal because the King and Queen of England visited here once."

At Eaton's department store, they bought new socks for

the boys, and a vest for Papa. Then Auntie Marie-Rose wanted to stop at the hat department.

"Now, Marie-Rose, you don't need a new hat," Auntie Claudine said.

"But you must admit this one is so chic." Auntie Marie-Rose patted on a shiny grey pill-box-style hat and peered at her reflection in the mirror above the display.

Sophie thought the hat looked like a large fish tin, except for the veil that Auntie Marie-Rose pulled over her eyes.

"No, no." Maman shook her head. "It's really not you."

Auntie Marie-Rose reluctantly returned the hat to the rack and followed them upstairs to the school uniform department.

By the time they'd bought all Sophie's school uniform for St. Ann's Academy — a tunic, a couple of long-sleeved white shirts, a red tie, some knee socks and a navy trench coat and tam — Sophie was starting to wilt.

"Time to stop for refreshments," Maman announced, and led the way down the stairs to the coffee bar on the lower floor. There were no vacant tables so they sat on bar stools at a long shiny counter. Maman and the aunties had donuts and coffee in thick white cups and Sophie had the smoothest and tastiest treat in her life, a chocolate malt. She spooned in a mouthful and let the cool sweet treat melt before swallowing it. Yum! It was so delicious she forgot for a few minutes about how nervous she was about going to the new school.

Then she remembered and frowned. She picked at a broken thumb nail.

"Why so sad, *cherie*?" Auntie Marie-Rose asked her. She was sitting next to Sophie. "You're not really worried about the new school, are you?"

"Well, um. It's just that I won't know anyone. All my school friends from last year will be going to Como Lake High."

"I know exactly how you feel." Auntie Marie-Rose nodded. "A new school can be a scary place. But you know what? I bet half the girls will be feeling as nervous as you. So you have to make the first move. Just go up to someone, especially someone who's looking shy and scared, and say, 'Hi.' For sure they'll say, 'Hi,' back. And before you know it, you'll have made a new friend."

Sophie thought that sounded way too easy, but maybe she'd try it on the first day.

"I have something else for breaking the ice." Auntie Marie-Rose rummaged through her parcels and pulled out a small paper bag that she handed to Sophie.

Sophie hesitated.

"Open it," Auntie Marie-Rose urged her. "Open it now."

Sophie peeked inside the bag. She pulled out a small book with a blue cover on which "Autographs" was printed in fancy gold letters. "Oh, thank you," she said, flipping through the pages. They were all different colours, pink, green, white. "It's beautiful."

"So this is something else you can do," Auntie Marie-Rose told her. "On that first day, go up to different people and ask them for an autograph. Everyone likes giving you their autograph."

"How about you writing the first one?" Sophie said.

"Gladly." She found a pencil in her purse and wrote:

> *Dear Sophie,*
> *Hope your life is like arithmetic —*
> *Happiness added*
> *Sorrows subtracted*
> *Friends multiplied*
> *And Love undivided.*
> *Your loving aunt, Marie-Rose*

"What's that?" Auntie Claudine leaned over and asked. "Oho! An autograph book! What a good idea."

"Would you like to write in it too?" Sophie asked her.

"Love to! Let me borrow your pencil, Marie-Rose." Auntie Claudine wrote,

> *Dear Sophie,*
> *Hope you'll be so famous.*
> *Hope you'll be a star.*
> *Hope you get to drive*
> *A really Big Red Car.*
> *Love from Auntie Claudine*

Auntie Marie-Rose laughed. "That reminds me of the story about what happened when Barbara Ann Scott came home from the World Figure Skating Championships in Europe with her gold medal."

"What happened?" Sophie asked.

"There was a big parade in Ottawa, right down the middle of Sparks Street, led by Prime Minister King, and Barbara Ann was riding on the back of a shiny yellow convertible. She was wearing her skating costume, and around her neck she had the big gleaming gold medal she'd won at the World Championships. Everybody in town was out there to see her, cheering and clapping and waving and she waved back to them. Oh, the crowds were so proud of her. Then at the end of the parade, she was given the yellow convertible as a gift. When they interviewed her on the radio, she said it was the happiest day of her whole life. It was just beautiful."

"It was beautiful," Auntie Claudine said. "Until they made her give the car back."

"Oh no! They made her give the car back?" Sophie said. "That's so terrible. Who would be so mean?"

"The Olympic committee. When they found out the town had given her a car, they said it would ruin her amateur status. They said she had to give back the yellow convertible, or give up competing for the Olympics."

"So what did she do?" Sophie asked.

"What could she do? She gave back the car. But then she said it was the saddest day of her life."

"And the next year, after she won the gold in the Olympics in Switzerland, she decided to become a professional skater," Auntie Marie-Rose said. "And you know what? They gave her back the car!"

"Look at the time!" Maman said. "We'd better be on our way."

They gathered up their parcels and left the store.

As they were strolling toward the car, they passed the Columbia Movie Theatre. A big poster declared, *Coming soon: "Annie Get Your Gun," starring Betty Hutton as Annie Oakley and Howard Keel as Frank Butler.*

"Oh, we absolutely must come back to town and see that. I bet it's a great movie," Auntie Claudine said. "I just love that Howard Keel. What a voice! And he's so handsome. Hubba-hubba!" She twitched her eyebrows at Sophie.

Sophie laughed, then another billboard on the other side of the movie theatre's glass doors caught her eye. "Look!" She grabbed Auntie Marie-Rose's arm. *"The World-Famous Hollywood Ice Review, starring Olympic gold medallist, Barbara Ann Scott. Coming soon!"* she read out in a loud excited voice. "Can you believe it? Barbara Ann Scott is coming here! To New Westminster!"

The poster showed a beautiful, smiling Barbara Ann Scott skating with her arms outstretched and one leg extending behind. She was wearing a short blue skating costume trimmed with white fur and she was surrounded by stars.

Behind her, in the shadows, was a man dressed in a dark sweater and pants. His arms were out, ready to support her.

"The World-Famous Hollywood Ice Review at Queen's

Park Arena for one week, September 9th to 16th, 1951," Sophie read, her heart flip-flopping. "And look what else it says. *'We'll be welcoming local talent. Chance of a Lifetime. Skate with the Stars.'* Imagine having a chance to skate in the Hollywood Ice Review! But what I would like most of all is to see Barbara Ann Scott skate in real life! And wouldn't it be so amazing to get her autograph in my new autograph book?" She squeezed her autograph book to her chest and glanced up at Auntie Marie-Rose.

But her aunt wasn't looking at Barbara Ann Scott. She was staring intently at the man in the shadows skating behind her.

"Do you know that skater?" Sophie asked her.

"Know him?" Auntie Marie-Rose shook her head. "No, no, no."

Somehow, Sophie didn't believe her.

It was warm that night after supper, so they opened wide the windows in the living room and gathered around the piano as Maman played and Marie Rose sang the old songs and some new ones as well. Finally everyone went to bed.

Sophie was stretched out on the sofa and, just as she was falling asleep, she heard them. The unmistakable grumble of motorcycle motors. It was hard to tell how many motorcycles there were and she was too sleepy to get up and go to the window to see. They rumbled past the house, their headlights flashing against the drawn curtains.

That night the menacing grumble and rumble of motorcycle motors haunted her dreams. She dreamt of huge herds of buffalo stampeding across the prairie chasing her, coming closer and closer. And her feet were stuck in cement and she couldn't lift them to escape.

6

First Day at the
New School

SEPTEMBER 4, 1951

"I want all grade seven girls in a line over here," directed a plump, pale-faced nun with a big nose. She was wearing a stiff white wimple around her face and a long black dress. A large silver crucifix dangled from her neck on a black string. "And grade eight girls over there. Straight lines, girls. Nice and straight. And silence, girls, now the bell has rung. I said, silence!"

Sophie was nervous. She'd managed the bus fine, getting off at the bus stop that Maman had shown her, right after the Pattullo Bridge. She had climbed the hill to the grey stone school behind a couple of other girls also dressed in navy tunics. They were older and hadn't glanced her way, so she had followed them shyly, her eyes on the steep path.

She stood in the grade seven line and fingered her new autograph book in the deep pocket of her new trench coat. It was really too warm for a coat, but since it was part of the school uniform, she was wearing it. Her back prickled with perspiration. She would have chewed her fingernails if she'd had any left to chew. The night before, she'd used Auntie Marie-Rose's file to file her ragged nails as short as they'd go.

There was a lot of jostling in the line and Sophie stepped back onto a girl's foot.

"Ouch!" the girl squawked.

Sophie jumped. "Oh, sorry," she whispered. "I didn't mean to step on your toes."

"Didn't really hurt." The girl shrugged. She had long red braids and lively green eyes behind thick glasses.

The plump nun glared at them.

Sophie pressed her lips together but she caught a glimpse of the girl winking at her and grinning. Before Sophie had a chance to smile back, the nun commanded, "Forward, march!" and, like a commander-in-chief, she led the grade seven line up worn stone steps, through tall glass doors and into the convent.

The hall was dimly lit with round lamps suspended from the high ceiling. Polished grey linoleum covered the floor, and dark-framed pictures of nuns and priests and bishops and sad-eyed saints with pale halos decorated the green walls.

Sophie followed the other girls along the hallway, through a door and into a narrow room lined with rows of metal clothes hooks.

"Hang your coats here," the teacher directed.

Sophie hung her coat next to where the girl with the red braids was hanging hers, but she didn't dare say anything. The nun led them into a stuffy classroom that smelled of chalk dust and musty clothes.

One of the classroom walls was a bank of windows, all tightly shut, in spite of the warm day. There were five rows of wooden desks connected to each other where the seat of one formed the front of the one behind it. Sophie hurried to the row beside the windows and grabbed the desk behind the girl with red braids. When the teacher read out the roll call, she discovered the girl's name was Mary Ellen Flanagan.

"My name is Sister Mary Hortense," the nun told the class, writing her name on the blackboard in big round letters. "And these are the rules of this classroom. First, there will be no talking in class whatsoever, unless you have been given permission. Second . . ."

The morning passed in a haze of school rules, recited by the teacher, then the handing out of textbooks they had to cover with special paper covers. Everyone else seemed to know exactly how to cut and fold the covers and attach them neatly to their textbooks, but Sophie had no idea how to do it. The outsides of her books were a mess with lop-sided corners and loose edges.

But the insides were something else. Flipping through the intriguing pages, she inhaled their sweet new-book smell. She especially liked the social studies textbook, *Ancient Civilizations*. It was filled with photographs of pyramids and coliseums and maps from the world of long ago. Before she could read much, the bell rang for recess.

"Line up at the door," the teacher barked. "And remember, girls. No talking until you are outside."

Sophie lined up with the rest of the girls. She didn't have a chance to go back to the cloak room to get her autograph book from her coat pocket.

The teacher led them in a silent single file along the dim hallway and out to the playground. "Now, girls . . ." She clapped her hands to get their attention. "I am leaving you alone for recess time, but I expect you all to behave as polite and respectful young ladies. And a reminder. You must never, ever, leave the school grounds during recess or lunch hour unless you have special permission. Is that clear?"

Sophie nodded with the other girls. The nun left them. And the girls drifted away to gather into tight knots of animated conversation.

Sophie stood alone. All the other girls seemed to know each other. Probably they had attended this school last year. Or maybe they'd come together from some other school close by. No one glanced in her direction, so she didn't have the courage to talk to anyone. She thought of what Auntie

Marie-Rose had told her. "Just go up and say, "Hi." Ask someone to write in your autograph book."

But since Sophie's autograph book was still in her coat pocket in the cloakroom, she didn't have it for an ice-breaker. She glanced away from her classmates.

There was a row of six swings. Most of them were unoccupied. Sophie sat on one and pushed herself slowly, back and forth. She peered around at the unfamiliar faces.

If she went up to any of them, they'd probably turn their back on her.

If only she knew one single person to talk to.

Her stomach was churning and she felt sick.

Maybe she should find the washroom and wait there until recess was over. Where was her Star Girl courage when she needed it?

"Race you!" challenged a girl, grabbing the next swing. It was the girl with red braids. Mary Ellen Flanagan.

"What do you mean, race?"

"Take four big pumps, then jump off. The one who jumps farthest, wins."

"Okay." Sophie grinned shyly at her and pulled her swing back until she was standing beside Mary Ellen. Sophie hung onto the cold chain links, her bottom on the canvas seat. She was ready to jump on and pump her hardest.

"Ready, set, go!" Mary Ellen shouted and took off.

Sophie thumped onto the seat, then pumped hard. The breeze swirled past her face and neck.

"One," Mary Ellen shouted, pumping hard, as well. "Two. Three. Four."

By then Sophie was swinging so high that at the highest point, the swing bounced.

"Jump!" Mary Ellen directed.

Jump from the swing, way up here? Sophie had to gather her Star Girl courage. She took a quick breath, let go of the swing and leaped off. She tumbled to the sandy ground and landed on her bottom with a thump. Before she could get up, the swing had swung forward again and smacked her squarely on the back of the head.

"Ow!" she yelled, clutching her throbbing head. She glanced over at Mary Ellen. Mary Ellen was on her feet, well out of the way of her swing. She'd jumped much further than Sophie had.

"I won that one," Mary Ellen said. "Want to go for the best of three?"

"Sure, I guess." Sophie rubbed her head and got back onto the swing. "How do you keep from falling back?"

"You have to start jumping off when the swing is moving forward. Not when it's at its highest point. Try it this time."

"Okay."

"Ready. Set. Go!" Mary Ellen shouted.

Sophie jumped on and pumped even harder. This time, the swing went so high, it felt as if it was swinging higher than the bar.

When Mary Ellen shouted, "Four!" Sophie pushed herself

off the swing. The thrust of the swing torpedoed her forward and up. For a second it felt as if she were shooting through the air. Like Star Girl with a Star Girl cape ruffling behind her. This time she landed on her knees in the soft sand. She looked over to Mary Ellen. Mary Ellen was still ahead, but this time, by only inches.

"Let's make it three out of five," Sophie yelled. "I bet I beat you next time."

"All right!"

Sophie's heart was thumping hard, as she waited for Mary Ellen to shout "Go!"

This time Sophie pumped with all her might.

When Mary Ellen shouted, "Four!" Sophie thrust herself forward, arms outstretched. For a second she had that fabulous feeling of flight again. She soared through the air.

"Star Girl!" she yelled as she landed even further.

She glanced over to Mary Ellen. This time Sophie had jumped almost as far as her.

"Star Girl?" Mary Ellen asked, breathlessly. "You mean Star Girl, like in the comics?"

"Um, yes," Sophie said, hoping Mary Ellen wouldn't think she was babyish or stupid.

"I love Star Girl!" Mary Ellen said. "I've got piles of her comics."

"Me too," Sophie said, relieved. "Just about every one that's ever been printed."

Her knee socks and tunic were all sandy so she brushed them off. Sand was even in her underwear. No one was looking, so she started brushing the sand out of her underwear as well.

Their teacher appeared from nowhere.

"What on earth have you two been up to? How did you get so dirty and dishevelled? Didn't you hear me say that you were to behave like young ladies during recess?"

"Yes, Sister." Sophie patted her tunic down over her knees so the nun wouldn't notice how sandy her knee socks were.

"And you, Mary Ellen Flanagan. You were here last year. You know the swings are off limits for you big girls. They're only for the little ones. In future, I expect much more ladylike behavior from you both," she said staring at Sophie.

"Yes, Sister," Sophie mumbled, her eyes on the ground. But now she'd discovered that jumping off swings was so invigorating, it would be awfully hard to stay away from them.

"Yes, Sister," Mary Ellen mumbled as well. Her cheeks were bright pink but when the nun turned away, her freckled nose twitched as she grinned at Sophie.

At lunchtime they ate in the classroom, then went out to play again in the playground. This time Sophie remembered her autograph book so she could ask Mary Ellen to write in it, but she didn't take it out of her tunic pocket because Mary Ellen was too busy. She'd brought her new Kodak Brownie camera to school and the other girls in the class wanted her to take their photo as they posed beside the trees.

None of the other girls glanced Sophie's way. Maybe she'd

go and wait in the washroom until lunch hour was over.

On her way inside, she passed the row of swings. One was free. She just couldn't stay away from them. It was such a rush of excitement to leap off and soar through the air as the swing thrust her forward. If she practised, she'd soon jump as far as Mary Ellen did, she just knew it.

She scanned the playground for their teacher. When she didn't see her or any of the other nuns, she sat on the vacant swing and pumped herself forward hard. One, two, three, four! She pushed off and flew through the air, further than she'd ever gone before. She landed on her feet in the sand with a thump. The force of landing propelled her forward to her knees, and her tunic flipped up the back.

"Sophie LaGrange! What do you think you're doing!" Sister Mary Hortense demanded, her long red nose pinched with anger.

Oh, oh. Caught again.

"Now how many times do I have to tell you, young lady, that when you are in grade seven, you are expected to behave in a mature ladylike and mannerly fashion." The nun shook her finger at Sophie.

Mary Ellen bounced in from nowhere. "Smile," she chirped and snapped a photo of the angry nun.

"What?" the nun shouted at her. "How dare you take a photo of me! Give me that camera at once, you impudent child!"

"Oh, Sister! I didn't even see you there." Mary Ellen

blinked innocently up at the nun and held the camera behind her back. "I was just taking a photo of my new friend."

"Yes, she was just taking a picture of me." Sophie nodded hard. "Truly, Sister. That's all she was doing."

"Sister Mary Hortense!" another nun called her. "Someone is here to meet you."

The nun composed her angry face. "Yes, Sister?" She turned from the girls and hurried away to meet a visiting priest.

The bell rang soon after and everyone ran to line up at the door.

"Thanks for saving my bacon," Mary Ellen whispered to Sophie as they joined the other grade sevens.

"Thanks for saving mine," Sophie hissed back.

7

Sophie's Close Encounter

THAT AFTERNOON, SOPHIE had to take the bus home alone because she'd had a detention. A detention on the first day of school. What a way to start the school year! All because she'd played on the swings after the teacher had told her not to.

Trudging up the hill on Blue Mountain Road from the bus stop, Sophie decided to take a shortcut along the gravel lane behind the houses. It was lined with ditches, weedy trees and shrubs and tall grass. Before she had reached the garage at the end she heard the menacing growl of a motorcycle's motor. One of the doors was ajar. "S.R.M.C." was carved into the wood on the inside of the door. The Satan's Rebels gang!

She peeked into the garage's dim interior where she saw three people in the shadows, tinkering with a motorcycle, revving its motor. Three bikers wearing black leather jackets. She leaned in further to hear what they were saying.

"They came into town last night on the train," said a rough voice.

"So why didn't you guys grab the dame then?" snarled an even rougher voice.

"Look, Lucifer. We couldn't. Too many people around at the train station. Guards and like that."

"I say we wait until she's alone, like at the ar—" The guy's eyes flicked to the doorway where the light caught his face.

Sophie gasped. Broad shoulders, dark eyes, long black curly hair! It was the biker who'd forced Joseph and her off the road last week.

"What the —? Why, you scummy snoop!"

He'd seen her! The biker had seen her!

He grabbed the motorcycle's handlebars and leaped onto it, revving it up.

Sophie bolted away, her heart racing. She leaped over the ditch and plunged into a thick cedar hedge, wriggling under it.

Both garage doors exploded open and the motorcycle growled out into the lane. The biker seemed to hesitate. He wouldn't know which way she'd gone.

Sophie squirmed around and peeked out from behind the hedge.

The bike was big and black.

It was coming toward her. Closer. And closer.

She pressed herself down into the dirt.

The bike roared past. But then it slowed down.

Now it was stopping!

The bike was looping back!

The driver peered around. Yes, that was him, all right. The same biker who'd run Joe and her off the road. What had the other biker called him? Lucifer?

Had he seen her duck under the hedge?

She held her breath and her heart pounded.

What would he do if he caught her? Beat her up for being a nosy snoop?

She peeked out again.

He was still there astride his motorcycle. He was staring right at the hedge.

Crouching, she backed away and scuttled across a scrubby back lawn. She glanced up at the house. Shut curtains. Probably no one home. No one to help her.

Keeping low, she snuck along a narrow path between the house and the side fence to a small front yard with a tall fence. There was a gate. And it led to the sidewalk.

She hurried out of the yard and up the sidewalk, peering around from behind shrubs. Traffic swished by, but no motorcycles.

Before she got to the next block, she heard the menacing throb of the motorcycle again. It was coming from the other side of the houses. Maybe the biker would turn down this road. And grab her!

She listened hard, her muscles tense, ready to escape into someone's yard again. But the sound of the motor faded until eventually it died away. The biker must have gone the other way.

Sophie continued sneaking along the sidewalk to the next road where she stared left and right. No motorcycle in sight. She took a deep breath, darted across the road and ran up the lane.

Finally she reached her own backyard. She tore up the back steps, pushed open the kitchen door and burst in.

"Sophie!" Maman said from the sink where she was peeling potatoes. "What's wrong? You're all out of breath. And you're so late. I was getting worried."

Sophie collapsed into a chair beside the kitchen table, panting.

Joseph was sitting on the other side of the table with Arthur, eating an after-school snack. Joseph stared at Sophie, his eyes concerned.

"Nothing's wrong." She shook her head and tried to take a deep breath. "I'm okay." She shrugged at him. She wanted to tell him about the scary encounter with the Satan's Rebels biker and what she'd heard, but she couldn't in front of Maman.

"How was your first day at school?" Maman asked her. "Did you make any new friends?"

Sophie peeled off her dusty trench coat. She was sweating and her shirt clung damply to her back. "Yes." She nodded. "One girl."

"That's nice. What's her name?"

"Mary Ellen. Takes the same bus as me, she said."

"Good. I'm glad you won't have to ride the bus alone. Where does she live?"

"Up the hill. Somewhere on Austin."

"You should invite her over after school one day. I'd like to meet her."

Joseph poured a glass of water from the pitcher and gave it to Sophie.

She nodded thanks.

"You'll never guess who I saw this morning at the arena before my hockey practice," he said.

"Who?" Sophie asked, after taking a gulp of cool water.

Barbara Ann Scott. You should see her!" Joseph said. "It was like she was actually flying or floating around on that ice. And those fantastic jumps and spins! She even did a bunch of sit spins."

"Sit spin?" Arthur asked. "What's that?"

"It's where you spin around and your spinning leg is bent like this at the knee and your other leg is extended forward." Joseph demonstrated in the middle of the kitchen. "Pretty tricky. She did lots of other figures too. Flying spins, forward and backward crossovers, even spirals. Best skater I've ever seen. Lots better than any of those skaters I used to take lessons with in Montreal. No wonder she won the gold medal at the Olympics. She's so-o classy." He smiled and his dark eyes went all dreamy.

Arthur wiggled his eyebrows at Sophie, making her giggle.

"You're so lucky, Joe," she said, helping herself to a piece of cinnamon toast from the stack on the table. "I'd give anything to see her. Maybe even shake her hand and get her autograph in my new autograph book."

"Maybe you'll get a chance," Joseph said. "I heard the skaters will be practising at the arena every day for the rest of the week before they put on that Hollywood Ice Review show next week."

"I'd so love to go to the show," Sophie said, biting into the cinnamon toast's sweet crunchiness. "Can we get tickets, Maman?"

"Oh, I don't think so, *chérie*. They're very expensive, and I've just spent all that money on your school uniform. And with the extra school fees and equipment and everything, there's not much money left over this month. I just don't know how we could ever afford tickets to the ice show."

Sophie's heart plunged with disappointment. Imagine someone as world famous as Barbara Ann Scott coming to New Westminster, and she wouldn't even get to see her!

"But it's my one chance to meet her, probably in my whole life," she cried, kicking the rungs of her chair.

"I'm sorry, Sophie." Maman shook her head. "We just don't have the money for such extravagances."

Sophie dragged herself into the living room. After wiping her sticky fingers on her tunic, she took her Barbara Ann Scott doll down from the piano and stared at it. She rocked it up and down to watch its shiny blue eyes open and close.

There must be some way she could get to see the real Barbara Ann Scott. She thought and thought and thought. She thought so much about how she could see the famous skater that she forgot to tell Joseph about her scary encounter with the Satan's Rebels biker.

8

Sophie's Plan

BY THE NEXT MORNING, Sophie had a plan. A good plan. Now, if only her new friend, Mary Ellen Flanagan would go for it.

Mary Ellen was already at the bus stop down on Brunette Street when Sophie arrived at eight fifteen.

"Have you ever heard of Barbara Ann Scott?" she asked Mary Ellen.

"Course. Everyone has. She's probably the most famous skater in the entire world."

"Did you know that she's here in New Westminster this week and next?"

"No, really? I'd love to see her. What's she here for?"

"For the Hollywood Ice Review. It's going to be on next week at Queen's Park Arena and she's the star. I saw a poster about it when we were shopping downtown."

"Wow! Someone so famous, right here in New West! The arena's just up the hill from school," Mary Ellen said. "I'd love to take a photo of her with my new camera and maybe sell it and make scads and scads of money."

"Especially if it was a photo *with* her autograph," Sophie said. "I have a plan."

The bus arrived then, so Sophie had to wait until they got on and found seats near the back. The bus was almost full and it smelled of shoe leather and diesel fuel.

"So what's your plan, Soph?" Mary Ellen asked as she nabbed a window seat.

"Okay. Here it is." Sophie sat down beside her. "My brother Joe said he saw Barbara Ann Scott practising at the arena yesterday morning before his hockey practice. She probably goes there to practise every day, so why don't we go and see her at lunch time? We have a whole hour and Queen's Park is not that far away from school."

"But we're not allowed to leave the school grounds during the lunch break."

"I bet we could sneak away and no one would even know we were gone. And we might actually get her autograph. That would be so neat."

"And I could take her photo?"

"You could take her photo."

"All right," Mary Ellen said. "Count me in!"

The morning's work at school really dragged. Math was a review of mixed fractions which Sophie had done every single year for at least the past four years. And spelling was writing out the new words five times each and making up a sentence with each one. Sophie tried to invent a story using all the words but her story didn't make much sense.

Finally the bell rang for recess.

"Looks like rain out there, so coats on, everyone, and line up at the door," the teacher said. "Remember. No talking."

Outside, the sky was heavy with grey clouds, but it wasn't actually raining yet. Sophie and Mary Ellen kept well away from the swings. They wouldn't attempt swing racing again. They didn't want to risk getting caught and having to do penance all lunch hour, which would ruin their plan for going to the arena. They just meandered around the school yard while recess stretched out to what felt like at least an hour.

This time Sophie remembered her autograph book. She asked her new friend to write in it. She'd even remembered a pencil.

"Sure, I'd love to," Mary Ellen said. "Where did you get such a pretty book?"

"One of my aunts gave it to me."

Mary Ellen wrote:

Dear Sophie,
Good, better, best.
Never have a rest
Until the good is better
And the better is best.
From your friend, Mary Ellen

"I like that, Mary Ellen. Thanks."

Sophie asked a couple other girls to write in the book too, which they did happily. Suddenly, she felt right in the middle of a tight clump of friendly activity. Her Auntie Marie-Rose had been right. Everyone loved writing in an autograph book. Her feelings of shyness began to melt away.

Just as it started raining, the bell finally rang.

After recess it was reading time, when they got to read the first story in their grade seven readers, *Canada's Early Pioneers.* Sophie liked the story about the early settlers in Quebec and how they'd cleared the pine forests from their land, then built log houses from the tall pine trees. It was fun to think that some of those people might even have been her relatives.

At the end of the story were a bunch of questions. Boring, boring, boring. She jotted down quick answers. Logs, By river, No, No, No, One hundred years ago, and Yes.

Then she flipped to the next story, "Boxcar Kid." It was an excerpt from a novel about a French Canadian family that had come west in 1909 and ended up living in a boxcar set on a side track right near her home in Maillardville. Now that sounded really interesting. She soon became so engrossed in the story that she wasn't aware of the teacher roaming up and down the aisle until she stopped at her desk.

"Sophie LaGrange," the nun said, "where are your answers for the questions?"

"Oh, um," Sophie muttered as she fumbled open her exercise book.

"Now that simply will not do." The teacher tapped her exercise book with her long pointer. "We always use full sentences for our answers in this class. Do it properly." The nun frowned at her then moved away and stopped at the desk of the girl who sat in the front seat. She was a large girl with long shiny ringlets, held back with a blue ribbon.

"May-Beth has done her work perfectly, as usual," the teacher said. "Now listen to this, girls. This is what I mean by a complete sentence answer." She stared meaningfully at Sophie, then read, "'The new settlers in Quebec built their homes with logs they had cleared from the pine forests around their farms.' Well done, May-Beth."

"Thank you, Sister," the girl murmured and shook her ringlets that wobbled like fat blond springs.

Sophie groaned. She'd have to do the whole exercise over again.

Finally, the bell rang. Sophie's heart leaped. This is it.

Mary Ellen turned around and grinned at her.

"From now on, on rainy days like today, you will eat in the lunch room downstairs," the teacher said. "Then you may play quietly there, or go out for some fresh air until the hour is over. You may collect your lunches and line up at the door. Quietly now, girls. Remember. No talking."

Sophie followed Mary Ellen to the cloakroom where they both grabbed their lunch bags. Then they were marched in single file with the other girls to a room in the basement of the school. It was a musty-smelling, dimly lit room with rows of tables and benches. The girls were supervised there by two elderly nuns who worked in the kitchen.

What if they were forced to stay down there in the basement for the whole hour, Sophie wondered. She and Mary Ellen wouldn't get a chance to sneak off to the arena.

"Please, Sister," Sophie said to one of the kitchen nuns, as the grade sevens filed past her. "May I go and use the washroom?"

"Certainly, dear."

Sophie raised her eyebrows at Mary Ellen.

"Me too," Mary Ellen said.

The nun nodded.

Sophie and Mary Ellen hurried down the corridor and ducked into the washroom. Empty. They peeked back out into the corridor. Empty now as well.

"There's a basement door that goes outside," Mary Ellen hissed. "This way."

Sophie followed her down another hallway where stern saints in dim paintings watched them with disapproving stares. A heavy door led outside and up a short flight of stone steps. It was raining lightly, but it wasn't cold.

"Coast is clear," Sophie whispered, peering around.

"Let's go!" Mary Ellen hissed back.

9

Queen's Park Arena

EXPECTING TO BE CAUGHT any second, the girls hurried across the empty school grounds, their heads pulled down into their shirt collars like turtles.

"Got your autograph book?" Mary Ellen whispered as they slipped out the swinging school gate.

"Right here." Sophie patted her tunic pocket. "And a pencil too. What about your camera?"

"Ditto." The small camera was on a strap around Mary Ellen's neck and tucked into the top of her tunic. The bulge it made on her chest was hardly noticeable.

Sophie glanced back at the school. No one was hanging around in the drizzle. So far, so good.

There wasn't much traffic on the road as they hurried across it. They hiked up a lane, munching their lunch sandwiches, then took a shortcut across damp grass through the park and finally reached the ice arena, a broad building with a gravel parking lot in front and along the side.

"Have you ever been in the arena before?" Sophie asked Mary Ellen.

"I went to a couple of hockey games last year with my dad," she said. "You?"

"No, but my oldest brother Joe comes here for hockey practice three times a week before school and on Saturdays. Where's the entrance?"

"On the other side."

They walked around the big building, only to discover the main entrance doors were locked.

"Rats!" Sophie rattled the door handle. "There must be some other way." She eyed the high windows.

"Don't even think of those windows." Mary Ellen shook her head. "We'd break our necks trying to get through them. I think there's a players' entrance on the other side of the building."

Past some bushes, they found a smaller door, much less obvious. And it wasn't locked.

Sophie followed Mary Ellen inside. It immediately felt cooler.

Sophie rubbed the damp sleeves of her shirt, trying to warm up. "Sure wish I'd brought my coat."

"Me too," Mary Ellen said. "But if we'd stopped for our

coats, Sister Mary Horney would have caught us, for sure."

Sophie shivered with cold and with excitement. She was so close to her idol, Barbara Ann Scott. Soon she'd see her. Then she'd have to muster up the courage to ask for her autograph. What if she said no? What if she was so snooty that she didn't give autographs to kids? What if she wouldn't even talk to them?

Sophie followed Mary Ellen along a dim corridor that led past some doors to dressing rooms. Then after it felt as if they'd gone around the whole arena, they found an entrance to the seating area. They climbed a long ramp to some bleachers that were covered with green wooden seats in rows up to the high dim walls around the ice rink. From there, they had a good view of the rink below.

Lights shone down on the ice, and on five or six skaters, whizzing around, skating backwards and forwards, leaping and dancing. Sophie held her breath as she stared down at the skaters, counting them. Three men and two women. But both women had dark hair, one short and curly and the other shoulder-length and tied back with a red ribbon.

"Can't see anyone that looks like Barbara Ann, can you?" Sophie's heart thumped with disappointment. "She has long blond hair."

Mary Ellen shook her head. "I don't see anyone who looks like her either."

Two more young women skaters came up the ramp to the bleachers. They were wearing warm sweaters and long pants, and they had skates tied around their necks. They stopped on the lowest bench beside a gate into the rink, to tie on their skates.

"Let's go and ask them when Barbara Ann Scott's coming," Sophie said.

"Okay." Marie Ellen followed Sophie down the steps.

"What are you girls doing here?" the taller skater asked them. "Playing hooky from school?" She had long dark hair, pulled back into a ponytail.

Mary Ellen shook her head. "No. We're on our lunch break. We just came to meet Barbara Ann Scott. Is she on her way?"

"Oh, the star of the show. No, she usually comes out first thing in the morning when the ice is really smooth to do her practice. And sometimes for a few hours in the evening as well, after they've run the machine over it."

The other skater said, "She needs perfectly smooth ice so she can practise all her jumps and turns. Some of them are pretty tricky."

Sophie swallowed back her shyness. "Sure would like to see her," she said.

"You'd have to get here awfully early in the morning, even before the hockey players do their practice, if you want to catch her." The taller skater smiled kindly at her.

"I wonder if I could have your autograph?" Sophie pulled her autograph book out of her pocket.

"Sure thing," the taller skater said. "But it'll be quick. Have you got a pencil?"

Sophie did. The woman flipped through the book and turned to a pink page. "So what's your name?"

Sophie told her and the woman wrote,

> Hi Sophie, ·
>> May your life always be as rosy as this page.
> Good luck, Sally Steele

The other woman turned to a pale blue page and wrote,

> Dear Sophie,
>> May you never feel like the colour of this page.
> Yours truly, Mavis Galley

"Gosh, thanks," Sophie said.

"Could I take your photo with Sophie?" Mary Ellen asked.

"Sure, kid, but like we said, we got to make it quick," the taller skater said. "We've got to get on the ice before our manager starts complaining. We're already late."

Mary Ellen flipped out her Brownie and pointed the camera at the skaters, one on each side of Sophie as they stood in a ray of sunlight from a high window. Sophie grinned at the camera and the shutter clicked.

"Thanks a lot," Mary Ellen said to the skaters.

"Good luck getting Barbara Ann's autograph," Sally said as they left for the ice.

"Look, it's already past 12:30," Mary Ellen said, pointing to the big clock over the rink. "We better get going or we'll be late."

Sophie led the way back down the ramp and into the dim corridor. "If we go that way, it'll be a shortcut and we'll get out quicker, right?"

"I don't know. We can try, I guess."

The corridor was like a wide tunnel around the whole arena. Eventually, it led to the main entrance, but the big doors were locked from the inside as well. So they had to retrace their steps, past the ramp that led up to the bleachers and back to the side entrance. By then, they'd broken into a run. Sophie slammed the door open and sprinted outside. Mary Ellen was right behind her. It had stopped raining but the sky was still overcast.

"Oh, boy. Sure hope we're not late for school." Mary Ellen panted beside Sophie. She had to hold onto her camera so it wouldn't bounce around so much.

They jogged across the parking lot.

"Hold on a sec." Mary Ellen stopped and took a couple of deep breaths as she wiped her glasses with the hem of her tunic and stuck them back on.

"We should hurry," Sophie said. "What if the bell's already rung?"

"Let's take a shortcut through the woods." Mary Ellen started running again and veered into the woods at the back of the arena, following an overgrown trail.

Sophie was right behind her.

10

Encounter with the Bikers

SOON THEY WERE SURROUNDED by bushes and trees whose branches hung damply over the path. Sophie ducked under a branch. She jolted to a standstill. "What's that sound?" she hissed.

Mary Ellen turned back. "What sound?"

Sophie held her breath and listened hard. "Can't you hear it? A motor. Up ahead." She hoped with all her might that it wasn't what she suspected. And that this trail wasn't leading right to it. "We've got to turn back." Her heart was hammering, and it wasn't from just the running.

"We can't," Mary Ellen panted. "We'll be late for school. Then Sister Mary Horny will know we left the grounds. And boy, will we ever get into big trouble. What's the matter?"

"Sounds like motorcycles up ahead."

"So?"

"So they might belong to the Satan's Rebels."

"Satan's Rebels? Who's that?"

"A motorcycle gang, and, and . . ."

"So it's a motorcycle gang. So what?"

"Listen, Mary Ellen. You don't want them to think you're spying on them."

"But we're not. We're just taking this shortcut back to school." She turned and jogged away.

"They won't believe you," Sophie called out to her back as loudly as she dared.

Mary Ellen shrugged as she disappeared around a bend.

What should Sophie do? What if those bikers caught Mary Ellen? She couldn't let her friend go off alone. She swallowed hard and followed her along the trail, catching up to her. Soon they came to a clearing about as big as her backyard. Some old broken-down equipment was strewn beside big puddles. Several bikers, mostly sitting on motorcycles and smoking, were hanging around mounds of gravel and sand. The air smelled of their cigarette smoke and motorcycle exhaust.

"This is the park's old gravel pit," Mary Ellen said. "I don't think they use it much any more."

Sophie ducked back into the woods. "That's the Satan's Rebels gang, all right," Sophie hissed to Mary Ellen.

"How do you know?"

"Look at the backs of their jackets. Satan's Rebels. Don't let them see you."

"Why not?"

"Because they're mean. And like I told you, they'll think we're spying on them."

"Look. If we don't take this shortcut, we'll be late for school and we'll get into so much trouble."

Before Sophie could argue with her any more, Mary Ellen burst right into the clearing!

Sophie wanted to run away. But she couldn't let her friend go alone, so she crept behind her, trying to stay hidden by the bushes.

No use. The bikers spotted them.

"So lookee here," one of them said, butting out his cigarette. "A couple of little chickies comin' to join up."

Other bikers swung around and stared at the girls.

Sophie's heart pounded. Holding her breath, she scanned their faces. When she didn't see the big biker with black hair, Lucifer, she let out her breath and stumbled after Mary Ellen who was marching right across the clearing, her head held high. She wasn't even glancing at the bikers.

"Whatever you do, don't run," Mary Ellen muttered back to Sophie. "If you do, they'll think you're scared."

A couple of bikers had turned their bikes and were heading over to them now, their motors throbbing menacingly.

"Don't be shy, girlies," one called out, as he drew nearer. "You're just what we've been looking for."

"Mary Ellen! Come on!" Sophie squealed, breaking into

a run. She grabbed Mary Ellen's sleeve and yanked her forward, toward the edge of the clearing.

Amazingly, Mary Ellen came with her and they both dived into the bushes and scrambled through the thick underbrush where no motorcycle could follow. As they dodged between the trunks of trees and leaped over logs and ferns, deeper and deeper into the bush, the sound of the motorcycles died away.

"I don't hear them now, do you?" Mary Ellen asked.

"No. I think we must be safe."

"How do you know about the biker gang?"

"My brother and me, we met them a few days ago. Then I saw them in a garage not far from my place. They're really mean. One biker chased me on his motorcycle."

Eventually, the girls burst out of the bush onto a road.

"Now what?" Sophie said, panting. "Do you know your way back to the school from here?"

"Sure. You see the river down there?" Mary Ellen pointed.

Sophie stared across the road and saw the glint of grey water in the distance between the houses.

"So if we keep heading down that way, we'll get to the school. But we sure better step on it."

By the time they got to school, the grounds were empty. No girls were strolling around among the trees or swinging on the swings.

"Oh no!" Mary Ellen cried. "I can't believe it! The bell must have already rung!"

"Maybe everyone stayed inside because of the weather."

"Some girls always go out, no matter what the weather's like," Mary Ellen said.

They dashed to a side door. Sophie tried to pull it open. "Shoot! It's locked."

"Let's try that basement door we used before."

Sophie scurried after Mary Ellen through the shrubbery to the other side of the school and down the stone steps. Mary Ellen yanked at the door.

"Crumbs! It's locked too."

"Are we ever in for it now," Sophie said, her heart thudding with apprehension.

"What a couple of dumb-clucks we are." Mary Ellen nodded. Her face was red and her bangs were plastered against her wet forehead. She rubbed an angry red scratch on her chin. "We're in real big trouble."

11
The Gym Class

"THE TEACHER. WHAT SHOULD we tell her?" Sophie asked
as they climbed back up the basement stairs and pushed
through the shrubs. She was breathing hard, trying to catch
her breath.

"I don't know," Mary Ellen whispered. She ducked into
the shrubs beside her. Her glasses were misted up again, so
she pulled them off and rubbed them with her thumbs.
"Maybe you have a sick grandmother? And we had to visit
her to be sure she'd eaten her lunch?"

"But that would be lying."

"True. Do you have any ideas?"

"No." Sophie shook her head and pushed through the shrubs toward their usual entrance. "We'll just have to face the music, I guess." Then she noticed a line of girls marching along the sidewalk that led from the main school building past the row of swings, to another building without windows. "Look! Isn't that Josie Mann from our class? And May-Beth?"

"You're right!" Mary Ellen said. "They must be on the way to the Annex for gym. I remember now. Sister Mary Horny said we're having gym after lunch. Talk about luck! We can just sneak in at the end of the line behind them."

Relief flooded through Sophie as she dashed across the school yard after Mary Ellen. They fell in step behind the other girls from their class. The girls at the end of the line glanced back at them, but they didn't say anything.

They filed into a building to a large echo-y room with high ceilings and a shiny wooden floor. The only furniture was a row of low benches along the sides.

The gym teacher was not a nun. "Good afternoon, girls. My name is Miss Peacock," a short woman wearing glasses announced in a high-pitched voice.

Sophie grinned at Mary Ellen and Mary Ellen grinned back. What luck! They were safe.

Miss Peacock said, "You may hang up your tunics on these clothes hooks above the benches and line up here in front of me in twos."

"What?" Sophie stared at Mary Ellen. "She expects us to

take our tunics off? Like, right here? Right in front of every-one?"

Mary Ellen looked as horrified as Sophie felt.

It soon became apparent that the other girls were all wearing gym shorts under their tunics, so they didn't mind pulling off their tunics and hanging them over the hooks.

In a panic, Sophie tugged her tunic hem down over her knee socks. So did Mary Ellen. What could she do? Sophie felt her face flush with embarrassment.

"Did you girls not hear?" Miss Peacock peered over her glasses at them.

"Um, I didn't bring my gym shorts today," Mary Ellen mumbled, her face red.

"Me neither." Sophie shook her head.

"Well, no matter," Miss Peacock said, in her squeaky voice. "I always have a few extra pairs of shorts that my dear mother has sewn for me for just such an occasion. But I don't often have a chance to use them. Don't know why, but I find students in my classes seldom forget their shorts."

She rummaged in a low cupboard and came up with two pairs of the most ghastly orange bloomers Sophie had ever seen.

"Hurry now, girls." Miss Peacock handed them each a pair. "Our time is a-wasting."

Out of the corner of her eye, Sophie noticed May-Beth and a couple other girls were giggling behind cupped hands at her and Mary Ellen.

Sophie turned her back and reluctantly pulled on the ugly orange bloomers under her tunic. She had no choice. The bloomers smelled musty and were huge. They'd have fit a large woman. She had to cinch the belt up tight around her waist so they wouldn't end up down around her ankles, and the front part bunched up in front of her stomach. Elastic around the legs gathered the fabric into two large orange balloons around her thighs. She pulled in a breath, yanked off her tunic and hung it on a hook beside Ellen's.

Her thighs had become a couple of fat wobbly pumpkins. When she tried to walk, the fat pumpkins rubbed against each other, making an embarrassing loud swishing noise. Swish, swish, swish. She tried to pull her shirt down over the bloomers, but it wasn't long enough.

Mary Ellen's face was bright red behind her foggy, steamed-up glasses.

Everywhere Sophie glanced, the girls were pointing and grinning at them.

"Come, come," Miss Peacock chirped to the class. "We need two nice straight lines. Now those lines are not straight. Come and join us, girls," she said to Sophie and Mary Ellen. "Don't be so shy now."

Sophie slunk to the end of one line, her pumpkin bloomers wobbling and swishing, and Mary Ellen slunk to the end of the other.

"Let's do some exercises first to limber us up." The teacher led them in a series of exercises. Jumping jacks and touching toes.

At least the other girls wouldn't stare at Sophie and Mary Ellen at the back of the lines.

Then the teacher cried out, "About face!" and everyone turned around.

Now Sophie was at the very front of her line, and so was Mary Ellen.

Everyone gawked at their wobbling pumpkin bloomers.

There wasn't a thing Sophie could do. She tried to concentrate on Star Girl, flashing through the air, her star cape fluttering behind her. And Barbara Ann Scott, in her glittering blue costume with the fur trim, gliding along the ice on shiny skates, the wind in her face, brushing her cheeks.

But Sophie couldn't block out the thought that every single girl in the class was giggling about how ridiculous she looked. She wished she could just disappear.

Then an even worse thing happened.

"Time for a game of dodge ball!" the teacher announced, clapping her hands. "Line one against line two, then we'll switch."

The orange pumpkin bloomers were the biggest target. Sophie was first out every time for team one. And Mary Ellen was first out every time for team two. The dodge ball was drawn to the hideous bloomers like a bumble bee to overripe pumpkins.

Sophie was just thinking this humiliating gym period would never end when the bell finally rang.

"That's it for this week, girls," Miss Peacock squeaked. "Put on your tunics and line up in your teams at the door.

Now, don't forget to return my shorts, please."

Sophie pulled her tunic down over her head and yanked off the ugly pumpkin bloomers. At last this embarrassment could end. She gave the bloomers back to Miss Peacock, muttering, "Thank you." So did Mary Ellen.

"Oh, you are most welcome, girls. I'm sure you won't forget your shorts again. Somehow, girls never do."

12

Mary Ellen's Visit

AFTER SCHOOL, SOPHIE took the bus home, as usual. This time Mary Ellen came with her. They got off at the bottom of the hill, and as they trudged up Blue Mountain Road, Sophie kept her eyes peeled for those scary Satan's Rebels bikers. She wasn't exactly scared to walk up the hill alone, but if one of those gang members came along, it sure was nice to be with a friend.

"Want to take a shortcut through the back lane?" Mary Ellen asked.

"No. I feel safer here on the main road," Sophie said.

They arrived at Quadling Avenue, where Sophie lived,

without seeing a single motorcycle. She was going to tell Mary Ellen about the biker gang, but what was there to tell? That a biker had chased her because she'd spied on them? Not much of a story there.

"Want to come over to my house for a while?" she asked Mary Ellen.

"Okay. But not for long. If I'm not home by four thirty my ma will worry. She always does."

When they came to her house, Sophie led the way around to the back. "Hello. I'm home," she called when they came in the back door into the kitchen. No answer.

There was a note on the kitchen table from Maman. "We've gone to visit Madame Comeau and will be back by five to make supper." And she'd signed it as she always signed her notes: *"Maman qui t'aime."*

"What's that mean?" Mary Ellen pointed to the French words.

"Love, Mom," Sophie said.

"Is your family French then?"

"Well, um, sort of. But we know how to speak English," she said in a rush, her face feeling hot with embarrassment. "Good English. All of us. Even my mom."

"That's neat," Mary Ellen said. "My parents are Irish. From Ireland, you know? And sometimes they say funny things like, 'Ye better be good or the wee ones will come and snatch ye away now.' Sure can be embarrassing when they do that in public. Know what I mean?"

Sophie smiled at Mary Ellen. She knew exactly what she meant. Family members could be very embarrassing sometimes. She knew then and there, that Mary Ellen was going to be her true friend.

After a snack of milk and peanut-butter cookies, Mary Ellen said, "These cookies are so delicious."

"My aunt Claudine made them," Sophie said. "She's training to be a pastry chef so she's always practising. Want to see my Barbara Ann Scott doll?"

"What? A Barbara Ann Scott doll? You have a Barbara Ann Scott doll? A real one? You lucky duck! I've wanted one of those forever. I'd love to see it."

Sophie led her into the living room.

"Oh my! She's just so beautiful!" Mary Ellen said. "I've never seen a Barbara Ann Scott doll in real life. Just heard about them. Can I hold her?"

"Course!" Sophie got the doll down from the piano and laid it in her new friend's arms.

"Gosh! She's got genuine leather ice skates and a silver tiara and everything."

"Even rollerskates." Sophie opened the tiny red box to show her.

"Wow! Did you get her for your birthday?"

"No. My aunts brought her from Montreal," Sophie said. "Sure wish we could see Barbara Ann in real life. I can't stand it that such a world famous person is right there in New Westminster, and we don't even get to see her."

"You're right, but what can we do about it?"

"I don't know yet, but I'll think of something. I just have to. Say, want to see my rollerskates? Or should we look at my Star Girl comic collection?"

"I don't think I have time to do both this time. Maybe the roller-skates?"

Sophie led Mary Ellen down to the basement.

"Oh, you have a skate key and everything!" Mary Ellen said. "Sure wish I had some rollerskates. Maybe I'll get some for Christmas this year."

"I got mine for my birthday."

"So can you skate?"

"A little," Sophie said.

"Let's see."

Sophie clamped the skates onto her shoes, tightened the front part with the key and buckled on the ankle straps. Then she skated around the basement, taking long smooth strides. She demonstrated how she could go backwards and turn around in loops.

"Wow! That's so great!" Mary Ellen clapped. "Can I try?"

"Sure."

Sophie showed her how to clamp the skates to her brown oxfords and helped her stand up. When Sophie let go of her arm, one of Mary Ellen's feet slid forward and the other slid back. She toppled over to her knees and her glasses fell off.

She'd never been on skates before, she said, not even ice skates. So although the roller skates had four wheels, it took a long time before she was able to stay upright without the skates sliding away from her.

"Try to just walk along," Sophie advised, hanging onto her arm again. "You can hold onto the posts and take little tiny steps until you get your balance."

Mary Ellen still had a lot of trouble.

Finally she took the skates off, and they each tried skating with just one skate.

"I like this a lot better," Mary Ellen said, scooting around the posts. "But I think I better get going. My ma will be wondering where I am and start calling the police. At least that's what she always threatens to do."

Sophie led the way upstairs and to the front door. As she was about to open it, there was a loud noise just outside. A motorcycle! It stopped in front of the house. Sophie's heart leaped. What if the Satan's Rebels bikers had discovered where she lived? And were coming to nab her?

She opened the door a crack and peered out.

"Oh, it's just my brother with his new motorcycle," she told Mary Ellen, and led her down the front steps.

Joseph was climbing off his motorcycle.

"Hi-ya, Soph," he said, taking off his goggles and helmet and brushing his dark hair away from his eyes. "Who's your cute friend?"

"Mary Ellen, from school. She's late so she has to get home quick."

"Hi, Mary Ellen." He grinned up at her.

Mary Ellen stared at Joseph, her eyes wide open. Her freckled cheeks flamed a deep red, and she opened her mouth, but the only sound to come out was a gurgle. She couldn't even say hi.

After a short uncomfortable silence, Sophie said, "Say, Joe. Could you give Mary Ellen a ride home? She lives up the hill on Austin. But she's kind of late, so her mom will be worried."

"Okee-dokee. I just have to get something from my room first." He hurried past them bounding up the front steps two at a time.

When he'd gone into the house, Sophie said to Mary Ellen, "What's the matter? You look like you've got a potato stuck in your throat."

Mary Ellen shook her head. Her green eyes behind her glasses were huge. "Oh, Sophie!" she said in a husky voice. "Your brother's so-oo cute. He's as handsome as a movie star. I've never in my whole entire life been so close to such a handsome fellow."

"What? Joe handsome? Oh, come on. He's my brother. And he's just, well, ordinary brotherly."

"I think he looks like . . ." Mary Ellen sighed, "just like Tony Curtis. No, he's even more handsome than Tony Curtis. He's so-o dreamy."

Sophie grinned and was about to tell her she was nuts when Joseph came back outside. "Climb aboard, kiddo," he said to Mary Ellen, as he got onto his bike.

Mary Ellen climbed onto the seat behind Joseph and held onto his waist. She was smiling as if she were in a trance. "Bye, Sophie," she whispered. "See you later."

Joseph revved up the motor and took off, trailing a cloud of dust and exhaust.

What was that all about, wondered Sophie. Mary Ellen surely was acting weird.

13

Sophie's New Scheme

FRIDAY NIGHT, AFTER supper of fried fish, mashed potatoes and slices of big ripe tomatoes, fresh from Papa's garden, Sophie had another idea about how she could meet Barbara Ann Scott. It was her turn to wash the dishes and Joseph's turn to dry. She was up to her elbows in suds when she got the brainwave.

"Thanks for giving my friend a ride home, Joe," she said.

"That's okay. I had to go up the hill anyway. She's a funny little duck, isn't she? When we got there, she just muttered something, maybe it was thanks, and scooted away into her house. She's sure a shy little kid."

"Mary Ellen shy? Gosh! I never thought of her as being shy. Anyway, are you going to your hockey practice tomorrow morning?"

"Course. Our first game is the week after next. We have to be ready. Can't afford to miss a single practice if we want to get into the provincial finals."

"And you'll be riding your motorcycle, right?"

"Yes. Why do you want to know all this?" He narrowed his eyes at her. "What scheme have you got up your sleeve?"

"Can I come to the arena with you tomorrow morning, Joe? Can I? I won't be any trouble at all."

"Why would you want to go to a hockey practice? Hey, I know. You've got your eye on one of the players. They're all too old for you, Soph. Way too old."

Sophie blushed. "No, course not. It's just that I'd so love to see Barbara Ann Scott. And you said that you saw her skating early in the morning, before your hockey practice when the ice is super-smooth."

"Why all this interest in Barbara Ann Scott?"

"Well, she's probably the most famous skater in the whole wide world. And here she is, right in New Westminster. So close. But Mom said that we can't go to the show because tickets are so expensive. Even if I did get to go to her show, I probably wouldn't actually meet her. This may be my only chance to see her up close."

"We'd have to get there even earlier than seven o'clock, which is when my hockey practice starts, you know."

"Before seven? Sure. What time would we have to leave here?"

"Before six, at the latest."

"If I could catch her at the end of her practice, that would be so great."

He shrugged. "You think Mom would let you ride on the back of the motorcycle all the way into town? Dream on."

"She didn't say anything when you gave me that ride around the block."

"Riding around the block is a lot different than riding all the way into town. Didn't you hear her? She thinks all motorcycles are machines of destruction, way too dangerous for anyone. She even wants me to get rid of it, which I think is completely ridiculous. Hey, are you washing those dishes, or not?"

"Um, sorry." Sophie quickly wiped the dishcloth over a plate and put it on the draining board, then she swished around in the suds to find some cups. Joseph was speedy about everything, including drying dishes. "Look. If Mom agrees that I can go with you tomorrow morning, will you take me?"

"Where would I put my hockey equipment? I usually strap it to the back seat."

"I could hold it on my lap. Then you wouldn't even have to strap it down. Right? Besides, you might even get a chance to meet Barbara Ann yourself."

She held her breath while he polished a drinking glass.

"Please, please, please," she muttered under her breath.

He stared at her, his dark eyes pensive. "Okay, I guess," he shrugged, finally. "But you have to convince Mom."

"Oh, I will, I will. I'll plan everything." She grinned at him. "Thanks, Joe. You won't regret it."

"You'll owe me a pretty penny after this." He grinned back.

After Sophie had finished washing the dishes and scouring the pots, draining out the water and scrubbing the white enamel sink until it sparkled, she went to find Maman. She was in the living room at the piano playing *"Vive la Compagnie,"* and Auntie Marie-Rose was singing along, *"Vive la vie, vive l'amour, vive la compagnie!"* They both finished with a flourish and laughed.

Auntie Claudine and Papa were playing cribbage.

Auntie Claudine slapped her cards down on the table. "Fifteen-two, fifteen-four, and a pair are six," she announced.

Zephram was the score keeper. Counting out loud, he moved the matchsticks carefully along the cribbage board.

Sophie stood beside her mother. "Could I ask you something, Maman?"

"What is it, *chou-chou*?" She was flipping through her music book to find another song. "What would you like to sing?"

"It's not about singing," Sophie said. "You know Barbara Ann Scott?"

"Of course." She glanced up at Sophie's doll still propped

on the piano. The sparkles in her dress caught the light from the piano lamp.

"Joe said that she practises early in the morning at the arena at Queen's Park before his team plays hockey."

"Yes? So?" Maman turned from the piano and gazed at Sophie, raising her eyebrows.

"I'd really like to go and see her skate, and maybe even get her autograph. And Joe said he'd take me tomorrow morning on the back of his motorcycle," Sophie finished in a rush. "Oh, please, please, please, Maman. Can I go?" she pleaded.

"What? You think I'd allow my only daughter ride all the way to New Westminster on the back of that dangerous machine! I'm nervous enough when that boy goes out alone." Maman shook her head. "No, no, *ma chérie*. I can't allow you to go."

"But, it's my one chance to see Barbara Ann Scott. And Joe's a very safe driver. Papa said so himself. Right, Papa?"

Papa glanced up from his cards. "It's true Joseph is a careful driver. But you must listen to your mother, Sophie."

"But, but, it'll be so early in the morning that there won't be any cars or trucks on the road, I bet."

Maman was still shaking her head.

"I know," Sophie said. "Joe can take you for ride around the block on his motorcycle right now, and you'll see what a careful driver he is and that it's really perfectly safe. It's just like riding a bicycle, except you don't have to pedal."

Joseph had finished drying the dishes and putting them away, and had come into the living room.

"Right, Joe? You can take Maman around the block on your motorcycle. Show her how safe it is?" Sophie asked him.

Joseph nodded. "Sure thing. You're the only one who hasn't had a ride on the new bike yet, Mom."

"And I never will, as long as I live. Those machines are much too dangerous. Every time you go out on that motor-cycle I worry and worry."

"But you shouldn't worry. You didn't ever worry when I was riding my bike to school, did you? It's the same thing."

"A bicycle doesn't go so fast," Maman said. "These days, every time you pick up the newspaper, there's a story about some boy getting killed on one of those dreadful machines. Oh, such a tragedy!"

"Most of those accidents are caused by kids fooling around with their friends on their motorcycles. Some of the kids don't even have a driver's licence. I'm always careful when I ride. Very careful. You should trust me." Joseph's voice was very quiet, the way it got when he was getting mad. His dark eyes sparked with anger.

Maman's voice was the opposite. She talked louder and louder, waving around her hands and her forehead was covered with worry lines.

"What about all those hoodlums you hear about joining those awful motorcycle gangs?"

"Hoodlums? Now you're saying I'm a hoodlum?"

"I just want you to be safe. You and Henri. And I don't think you two are safe, riding around on that dangerous machine."

Sophie could see that Maman was getting all worked up about motorcycles. Any minute now, she might forbid Joseph to ride his. She might even insist that he sell it immediately.

"Maman," Sophie said, pushing onto the piano bench beside her mother and flipping through the thick book of folksongs. "What about, "Au Claire de la Lune?" We haven't sung that one for ages. How does it go again?"

Maman sighed. She turned and smiled at her, looking happy for the distraction. She played a few chords on the piano. "I thought you'd know this one by heart." She nodded for Sophie to begin signing.

"Au claire de la lune, mon ami, Pierrot," Sophie started the old folk song.

Auntie Marie Rose joined her. *"Prête-moi ta plume . . ."*

By the time they finished the second verse, the lines of tension from Maman's face had disappeared.

And so had Joseph's.

14

The Motorcycle Ride
to the Arena

THAT NIGHT, SOPHIE couldn't sleep. It wasn't that the sofa in the living room was uncomfortable, it was the thought that tomorrow she was going to miss the one chance in her whole life to meet her idol, Barbara Ann Scott, probably the most famous skater in the entire world. She couldn't stand it! There must be some way that she could see her. There had to be.

She thought and thought and thought. Before falling asleep, she had come up with another plan.

The next morning, when she heard Joseph rustling in the kitchen, she popped out of bed and slipped on her jeans and a long-sleeved shirt. She pulled her blankets over her pillow and a couple of cushions so it appeared as if she were still asleep on the sofa.

She joined Joseph in the kitchen. He was at the table spooning cereal into his mouth from a big bowl.

"What are you doing up so early, Soph?" he asked.

"I still want to go with you to the arena this morning, Joe," she whispered to him.

"You heard what Mom said. She said no."

"She didn't exactly forbid me to go with you. She just said that she thought motorcycles were dangerous. Besides, she has that wedding at church this morning, so she won't even know I'm gone. Please, Joe," she pleaded. "This is probably the one and only chance I'll ever get to meet Barbara Ann Scott in my whole entire life."

He shook his head.

"And maybe you'd get a chance to meet her too," she persisted. "Maybe even talk to her."

"Don't think so, kiddo."

"Look. I won't be any trouble at all. I'll just be there at the back of your bike hanging onto your bag and stuff. You won't even know I'm there. How about if I clean your bike for you every day for the next week?"

He shrugged.

"Okay then, I'll do all your kitchen chores for the next month."

"Did you see what the weather's like out there? It's pouring."

Sophie pulled back the kitchen curtain and stared outside. It was still dark, but she could see in the street light's beam that it was raining hard. "Oh, no! It looks awful. Are you still going to your hockey practice, Joe?"

"Of course. Can't let the rain stop me. The practice is indoors anyway. And I told you. None of us can afford to miss a single practice if we want to make it to the provincial finals. But you'd get soaked on the back of the bike, Soph."

"That's all right. I'll wear my winter coat. And a hat. And a scarf. And mitts. Oh, please, Joe. I'll never ever ask you for anything ever again in my whole entire life. Please, please," she begged. "Plee-ease."

He sighed. Then he said, "All my chores for a month, eh?"

Sophie nodded. She was desperate.

Finally he shrugged. "Okay, but if they find out, you have to say you forced me to take you."

She grinned at him. "Don't worry. I'll take all the blame. But they're not going to find out anyway. Like I said, Mom has to play the organ for that wedding this morning, and she always leaves early enough to practise with the singers before the wedding starts."

Sophie's stomach churned with excitement. She couldn't get any breakfast down except for a few sips of milk. She felt like dancing across the kitchen floor and yelling Yippee! She was going to meet her idol after all.

She tiptoed into her darkened bedroom where her aunts were still sleeping and fished out an extra sweater from her dresser. Then she crept back to the kitchen and bundled up in her thick winter coat, tucking her autograph book into an inside pocket.

While Joseph went down to the basement for a canvas tarp to protect them from the rain, Sophie wrapped a long woolly scarf around her neck and face and pulled on her hat.

"Right," Joseph said, coming up from the basement with the tarp. "Ready?"

Sophie nodded behind her scarf. With all the extra clothes, she felt round and fat as a snowman.

"Let's go." He quietly opened the backdoor and slipped out onto the porch.

Sophie waddled down the back steps after him, trying to be as quiet as she could.

The motorcycle was in the garage in the back lane. Joseph had to help her climb up onto the back seat. She found the foot pegs with her feet. The cold of the leather seat seeped through her jeans, but she didn't say anything.

He gave her his bulky canvas bag of hockey equipment to hold on her lap, as well as his hockey stick.

"I have to hold all this stuff?" she asked, trying to hitch the hockey stick under her elbow.

"You said you would, remember?" He mounted the bike in front of her and tucked the canvas tarp around himself, then passed the edges back to her. "All right, kiddo?"

"All right, I guess," she muttered through the scarf. She

squeezed her elbow down to hold onto the hockey stick with one arm and clutched his bag with her other hand.

"Main thing is to keep the tarp from getting caught in the back wheel."

"Right." She nodded.

"Hang on tight now."

She grabbed the back of his leather jacket as they roared off into the early morning light, the canvas tarp flapping damply around them. She glanced up at their house as they rode away. All was in darkness. Everyone else in the family was still asleep.

Before they'd even left their neighbourhood, the cold damp wind had snaked its way up Sophie's sleeves and pant legs, and down the back of her neck. Shivering, she buried her face into Joseph's back trying to avoid the cutting breeze and freezing rain that lashed her cheeks like tiny whips. The wind pulled at the tarp, so she had to grab it with one hand and try to hold the equipment bag and hockey stick with the other. Now she couldn't hold onto Joseph! What if she fell off?

Wishing she had another hand, she clamped her knees around the seat as if she were riding a horse. The vibration of the motor jiggled her legs and her backside. The trees and houses flashed by in a damp grey blur. Riding on the motorcycle was like riding a live animal, like galloping along the wet streets on a spirited steed. Her feet soon became so numb with cold that she lost any feeling in her toes.

Joseph turned the motorcycle onto Columbia Street and the wind from the river blasted at the tarp, yanking it away. Letting go of the equipment bag, Sophie clutched the flapping tarp. They crashed over a hard bump and the bag bounced off her lap. She made a grab for it but it slid away from her grasp.

"Oh no! Joe! Your bag!" she yelled. "Your bag fell off!"

"What!" Joseph yelled back. He jammed on the brakes and the motorcycle skidded to a stop. "I thought you were holding onto it."

"I was. But — but . . . I'm sorry, Joe."

A big truck lumbered past, horn blaring at them. Sophie tried to duck under the tarp but an icy wave of water hit her head. She squealed, burying her face in her arm.

"Darn truck," Joseph grunted, as he untangled himself from the tarp and climbed off. He pushed the motorcycle to the edge of the road and kicked down the stand. "You stay here with the bike and hold onto this tarp, okay?" he said, tucking it around her.

He left her shivering on the motorcycle while he hiked back to retrieve his bag.

Another truck swished past, but this time Sophie had time to duck under the tarp before the cold spray drummed onto her head. Shivering, she waited for Joseph, and waited.

After a long time, he jogged back, carrying his bag.

"What took so long?" Sophie asked as he handed it to her. The bag was wet and muddy.

"At first I couldn't find it. Then I spotted it in the middle of the road. I think a truck ran over it. Sure hope it didn't damage my new skates. That's all I have to say."

Sophie hoped as well. She knew those skates were really expensive and Joseph had been so proud early that summer when he'd bought them with his first paycheque from his job at the mill.

"I'm really sorry, Joe," she said.

"I know you didn't do it on purpose, Soph." He got up on the motorcycle and wrapped himself and her in the tarp again. "Okay. Hang on real tight. And whatever you do, don't let go of that bag."

"Don't worry. I'll hold onto it, no matter what."

They took off and she gripped the seat between her knees. Every time a truck swished past them, the damp tarp flapped around her head, but she didn't let go of the bag for an instant, even when they went over a big bump and she bounced a few inches off the seat.

The rest of the trip on the road along the river, then up the hill to the arena, felt like hours.

Finally they rolled into the muddy parking lot. The motorcycle slowed down and bounced through the puddles. It was still quite dark out, and the arena lights shone on a few rain-slicked cars. A couple of other motorcycles were parked in one corner beside a telephone pole. Joseph rolled his bike beside them.

Sophie thought they probably didn't belong to the Satan's

Rebels gang members, but she wasn't sure. They were big and they were black. She stared into the bushes at the back of the arena but didn't see any sign of them.

"You okay, kiddo?" Joseph asked after he'd turned off the noisy motor, and pushed off the wet tarp. "You survived? Not too cold and wet?"

"I'm fine." Sophie said through chattering teeth. Now the ride was over, she was still shivering, but she actually felt great. Light and buoyant, and her cheeks tingled. She climbed off the bike and stamped her numb feet. Her legs felt like jiggly jelly from the motor, and her jeans were soaked. "Sure hope we got here early enough to see Barbara Ann," she said, holding Joe's equipment bag and hockey stick while he dismounted.

Joseph pulled off his goggles and aviation helmet and draped the tarp over his motorcycle to protect it from the rain.

Sophie gave him his hockey equipment and rubbed her trembling legs.

Joseph zipped open the bag and pulled out his skates, silver-coloured blades and polished black and brown leather.

Sophie caught her breath while he examined them.

"Looking good," he said, finally.

"Thank goodness for that," Sophie said.

"Let's go," he said, slinging his hockey stick and equipment bag over his shoulder.

15

Waiting for Barbara Ann

SOPHIE FOLLOWED HER brother to the side entrance of the arena, the same one she and Mary Ellen had used the day before. The long corridor was lit by dim lights way up in its high ceiling. She felt in her inside pocket. Yes, the autograph book was still there. And it felt dry. Good thing she'd put it into her inside pocket. Now, if only Barbara Ann Scott were still on the ice . . .

"This is the way to the hockey players' dressing room," Joseph told her. "You can't come in here. The closest entrance to the bleachers is down the hall that way. Just go up the ramp and you'll see the ice from there."

Sophie almost said, "I know," but she remembered she

wasn't supposed to have already been to the arena. She didn't want anyone to find out about the noon hour when she and Mary Ellen had played hooky from school to come here. Not even Joseph.

"See you later," she said, hurrying away to the bleachers entrance. She was nervous. What if Barbara Ann turned out to be so snooty that she wouldn't even talk to her?

Bright lights were shining down on the ice and, except for a few skate marks in the centre, it was mirror smooth. And empty.

Barbara Ann Scott wasn't there. No one was there. Darn! They were too late and had missed her. Probably all because she'd dropped Joe's bag and Joe had to spend all that time going back for it. Or maybe something had happened to her.

Maybe she was still in the dressing room. If there was a dressing room for hockey players, there must be one for fig- ure skaters.

Sophie rushed back down the ramp to the dim corridor. As she hurried past the hallway to the hockey players' dress- ing room, she almost bumped into two people emerging from a shadowy corner.

She gasped. They were wearing black leather jackets. Satan's Rebels bikers! What were they doing here at the arena, lurking in the shadows?

Sophie gulped hard and pulled the scarf over her face. Hoping they wouldn't recognize her, she hurried away to another hallway and a door. "Ladies," declared a sign above it.

She turned the door knob. The door was unlocked. She yanked it open and rushed inside, pulling it shut behind her. She didn't think the bikers would follow her here.

It was quite a big room, lit only by a bank of windows set high on the walls above a row of lockers. She searched for a light switch but didn't see one.

"Hello?" she called. Her voice sounded echo-y and scared. "Hello-o!"

No one answered. Barbara Ann Scott wasn't here either. If she'd even been here. Darn! Darn! Double darn! What rotten luck! Maybe she took Saturday morning off? Or maybe she'd be practising later? Or maybe they were too late and had missed her?

Sophie turned away, disappointed. A glint of something shiny caught her eye. Something under a low wooden table. What was it?

She picked it up. A bracelet! A shiny silver bracelet with a row of what appeared to be diamonds. Sophie turned it over and held it so the light from the windows could illuminate it. The back was engraved in fancy letters. The initials, BAS. Barbara Ann Scott! Sophie's heart leaped. Imagine! This must be Barbara Ann Scott's bracelet! She held it to her chest. Then she examined it more closely and saw the clasp was broken. It must have fallen off her wrist while she was changing.

What should she do with it? Sophie wondered. No one was around to give it to. Joseph wouldn't know what to do with it. Neither would the other hockey players or the coach.

Then Sophie knew exactly what she could do. She'd give the bracelet to Barbara Ann Scott herself. In person! That would be *so* terrific. Then she'd get to meet the famous skater and get her autograph. Her dream would come true.

But how could she find out where Barbara Ann was staying?

She stuffed the bracelet into her jacket pocket and peeked out of the dressing room. No one was in the hallway. She wasn't taking any chances of bumping into those bikers though. She pulled her scarf up around her face again and crept back to the bleachers to wait for her brother to finish his hockey practice.

She didn't meet anyone along the way and she was the only one in the bleachers, where she had a good view of the rink. The players had started now and were skating up and down the ice in a line, taking shots on the goalie while the coach yelled out instructions.

Sophie recognized Joseph right away. She thought he was the fastest skater on the ice, although a couple of other players could skate pretty fast as well. But her brother not only skated fast, his skating was smooth and graceful to watch. Elegant, she thought. But then, he'd been skating ever since he could walk. When they lived in Montreal, he'd taken figure skating lessons for years. He'd wanted to continue the skating lessons when they moved to BC, but he hadn't found a teacher, so he played hockey instead.

Sophie sat on the cold wooden bench. Her jeans were still uncomfortably damp from the wet motorcycle ride and her toes were numb. She stamped her feet, trying to warm them up. She shoved her hands deep into her pockets. Her autograph book was in one pocket. And in the other was the silver bracelet. She fingered its rough surface where the diamonds were.

She imagined Barbara Ann Scott's grateful smile when she gave it back to her. She would smile back and maybe even shake her hand. Oh, it was going to be wonderful!

The hockey practice took so long that in spite of all her layers of clothing, Sophie was shivering with cold right down to her bones.

Finally the coach blew his whistle. "That's it for today, fellows," he shouted.

The hockey players headed off the ice. Sophie got up and marched around a bit, stamping her feet some more and rubbing her hands together. No point going to the dressing room door to wait for Joseph yet. It would take him a few minutes to change. Also, those bikers might still be hanging around.

She heard a sound like paper being ripped. Someone else was skating. Had Barbara Ann Scott returned? Sophie swung around to watch.

It wasn't Barbara Ann. It was another skater. A man. This

one was definitely not a hockey player. He looked vaguely familiar. Right! Sophie nodded as she recognized him. The skater in the shadows on that poster of Barbara Ann Scott at the movie theatre.

In real life, he was truly a vision. Tall and slim, dressed all in black. Long black pants, a snug black sweater and black skates. And his long hair was black too. He glided over the ice so effortlessly, so smoothly and gracefully, spinning into swirls and carving out figures of eight that he was like a phantom on skates. He skated backwards as easily as forwards. And then he jumped and twirled, and jumped and twirled again, spinning round and round the ice, landing as elegantly as a ballet dancer, his arms outstretched.

Oh, my gosh! Sophie thought. It's like he's flying. Or floating on the air. She couldn't believe what she was seeing. Such beauty, such grace. She was totally transfixed, mesmerized. She imagined herself skating in his arms, twirling and whirling around the ice. She watched him for what seemed just a minute, but might have been an hour.

"Hey, Sophie," a voice called her. "Let's go."

Reluctantly, she pulled her eyes away from the vision on the ice. "The ice phantom," she whispered to herself and shivered.

Joseph was calling her from the ramp. "Come on, Soph. Let's go. We got to hit the road."

"Okay." She hurried to catch up to her brother who was striding down the long corridor and outside. "Do you know who that is?" she asked him.

"Who?"

"That skater on the ice now."

"The guy dressed in black? No. I've seen him on the ice after our hockey practice a couple of times before. Someone said that he's one of the lead skaters in the ice show they're putting on next week."

"Maybe he's Barbara Ann Scott's partner, do you think?"

"Maybe."

"Boy! He sure can skate! When he takes those jumps, it's like he's actually flying."

"Bet he's a lousy hockey player though."

"Maybe he'd give me his autograph. I'll go ask him."

"Not this morning, Soph. Let's get rolling. I got things to do." He pulled the tarp from his motorcycle and strapped on his goggles. "You coming, or what?" he asked, mounting his bike.

For a second, Sophie almost went back into the arena to get the skater's autograph. But if she didn't leave with her brother now, how would she get home?

She pulled her hat down over her ears and reluctantly climbed up behind him, holding his bag and hockey stick.

Joseph swatted back a corner of the tarp to her. "Don't drop the bag this time," he said.

"Don't worry. I won't."

He revved up the motor and they took off, the damp tarp flapping around them.

The other motorcycles that had been parked beside Joseph's earlier were gone now. Did they belong to the Satan's

Rebels bikers, Sophie wondered as she shut her eyes against the cold rain spraying up into her face. She leaned her cheek against Joseph's broad reassuring back.

The ride home wasn't as cold and windy as the ride there. Maybe because it was later and the sun was up.

Or maybe it was the thought of the handsome phantom skater. Thinking about him made Sophie feel all bubbly inside, like a glass of ginger ale. She couldn't wait to tell Mary Ellen about him.

A song started buzzing through her head, taking her completely by surprise: *"I've got my love to keep me warm . . ."*

She would have blushed if anyone found out about it.

16
Tracking Down Barbara Ann

WHEN THEY ARRIVED home, everyone was sitting around the kitchen table having breakfast, except Maman, who'd already left to play the organ at the wedding at church and Papa who had taken her in the car.

Auntie Claudine was at the stove, flipping french toast.

"There you are, Sophie. We thought you were sleeping in, but when Zephram went to wake you up, you were gone. You didn't go to the rink with Joseph, did you? Your mom won't be very happy about that, you know."

Sophie nodded. "I just had to go, Auntie. It was my one chance to see Barbara Ann Scott."

"So did you see her?"

"No, she wasn't there after all," Sophie said, pulling off her wet shoes and socks and stacking them on the radiator to dry. She was still buzzing with what she had seen on the ice. The Ice Phantom.

She shook off her thick coat and something fell out of the pocket and clunked to the floor.

"What's that?" Arthur asked.

"Oh, I almost forgot!" She picked up the bracelet. "I found this in the ladies' dressing room at the arena. And look, it's got initials on the back."

Arthur examined it under the kitchen light. "BAS," he said.

"Oh!" Auntie Marie-Rose said. "Barbara Ann Scott! You found Barbara Ann's bracelet! Let me have a look." Arthur gave it to her and she turned it over. "I wonder if these are glass or real diamonds. If they're real, this could be a valuable piece of jewellery. I'm sure she'd like it back."

"Maybe she'd even give you a reward for finding it," Arthur said.

"A reward!" Sophie said. "But how could I get it to her? I don't know where she's staying."

"We'll make some phone calls and track her down," Auntie Claudine said. "But here. Come and sit down. You two must be starving. Have this french toast before it gets cold."

Sophie sat on the long bench beside Zephram. Funny, she

just wasn't all that hungry. Usually she loved french toast with maple syrup more than anything. Somehow, she just couldn't get out of her mind the image of the beautiful phantom skater dressed all in black. He twirled and whirled and swirled around in her head.

After breakfast, she put her socks and shoes back on. They were still wet, but the radiator had warmed them. She went down to the basement, clamped on her rollerskates and pulled up her socks. Her jeans were still damp from the ride home, but as she wasn't cold, why bother changing them?

She fiddled with the dial on the radio until she found some smooth romantic music, then she started skating around the basement, thinking of nothing but that graceful skater. "The Phantom," she whispered to herself. "The tall, dark and handsome Ice Phantom."

Every stride she took, she thought of how he glided around the ice, one foot, then the other, around and around, and into loops and figure eights around again. So smooth, so beautiful, his dark hair flowing out behind him. She sang along with the dreamy music, making up the words: *"Skate, skate, across the lake, where the sun is glistening off the snow. Snow, snow, the snowy snow blows across the rolling hills . . ."* She skated away to another land.

"Sophie!" Arthur yelled down into the basement. His voice was so loud, it penetrated her dream world. "It's your turn to dry the dishes this morning."

Drat! "Okay, okay, I'm coming," she called.

Auntie Marie-Rose met her at the top of the stairs. Her cheeks were rosy and she was grinning.

"You'll never guess," she said to Sophie. "We called around and found out that Barbara Ann Scott is staying at the Royal Hotel downtown in New Westminster. So we're going there to give her back her bracelet. I just talked to her on the telephone and she actually remembers me from high school! Anyway, she's been so worried about her bracelet and hadn't realized that she'd lost it at the arena. And she wants to meet you, of course, to say thank you for finding it."

"Terrific!" Sophie's heart leaped. "When are we going?"

"We'll ask your dad if he can drive us after they get back with the car from the wedding."

Sophie hugged herself tight. Finally, she was going to meet Barbara Ann Scott! She hoped she was nice. And she hoped she'd have the courage to ask her for her autograph.

Way at the back of her mind, she had another thought. Wouldn't it be so wonderful if she could meet her phantom skater as well? But on the other hand, if she did meet him face to face, she'd probably be so excited, she'd melt into a puddle at his feet.

Now all they had to do was wait until Maman and Papa got home.

But what about Mary Ellen, she wondered. She knew that her new friend would love to meet the famous skater as well. But she didn't know where she lived, or her telephone number. Maybe her family didn't even have a telephone.

After she finished drying the dishes and stacking them away, she wandered into the living room and fiddled around on the piano, picking out tunes and humming along. She smiled up at the Barbara Ann Scott doll, still propped up on the piano. She couldn't believe it. Soon she'd be meeting the real person. The real live, world-famous Barbara Ann Scott! The doll stared back at her, smiling her little smile with her tiny white teeth glinting, her rosy cheeks dimpled.

The hours stretched out and her parents didn't return home. Sophie fished a pile of her Star Girl comics from under her bed and she and Zephram curled up on the sofa in the living room and read them.

The clock on the bureau chimed twelve. Their parents still didn't come home. The smell of soup drifted from the kitchen.

"Lunch is ready," Auntie Claudine called them.

Auntie Marie-Rose was setting the table. She had a scarf wrapped around rows of pin curlers on her head. "Joseph and Henri are in the back lane working on that motorcycle. Sophie, could you please tell them soup's ready?"

Joseph and Henri were bent over the motorcycle, rubbing it with oily rags, but they came for lunch when Sophie called them.

The chicken-rice soup was delicious.

"Can I have another bowlful?" Sophie asked.

"Sure, but leave some for your parents," Auntie Claudine

said. "I'm sure they'll be hungry when they get home."

After lunch Sophie kept running to the front window to check if Maman and Papa were there yet. It felt as if the afternoon stretched on for days. After a while she went downstairs to do some more roller skating, but she kept her ears open for sounds of her parents' return.

17

Meeting the Famous
Barbara Ann Scott

FINALLY SHE HEARD Zephram's steps running to the front door and him squealing, "Maman! Papa!" as if their parents had been gone for weeks.

Sophie kicked off her skates and scrambled upstairs.

Papa stayed out in the front garden to inspect his roses, while Maman came into the living room, taking off her coat. Her hat was askew and her dark blue dress wrinkled.

"Oh," she groaned, collapsing into her comfy chair and propping her legs on the stool. "That must be the most exhausting wedding I've ever been to!"

"What happened?" Auntie Claudine asked.

"Well, for one thing, the bride was almost an hour late so I had to keep playing variations of the wedding music on that wheezy old church organ. I don't know when they're going to get a new one. And then after the service, we had to wait forever for the bride and groom to come back from the photographer's."

"But why did you stay? You could have come home then."

"They needed me to play the piano during the reception in the church hall. And Papa helped by serving the wine."

"We saved you some soup. You must be starving."

"No, they gave us a very nice lunch, Papa and me. But now, I just want to keep my feet up for a while. Ah, that's better," she said as she took off her high-heeled shoes and kneaded her toes. "So did you get Barbara Ann Scott's autograph, Sophie?"

Sophie gulped and stared at her mother. "How did you know I went to the arena?"

"When I went into the living room to get my music for the wedding, I saw you were gone. And by then Joseph had already left for his practice. So I put two and two together."

Although her eyebrows were knotted, Sophie saw she didn't look really mad.

"I just *had* to go, Maman," she tried to explain. "It was my one chance ever in my whole entire life, to see her. And, and you didn't exactly say that I couldn't go with Joseph."

Maman shrugged. "You're very lucky I'm so exhausted, Sophie. I'm just too tired to be angry with you. But I'm disappointed you and Joseph would do something like that behind my back. That motorcycle of his is causing nothing but trouble. Do you know how worried I was about you?"

"Sorry, Maman." Sophie stared down at the carpet. She really did feel badly about disappointing her mother. "But you can't blame Joseph. It wasn't his fault at all. I made him take me."

"And you still didn't get to meet the famous lady?"

"No. By the time we got to the arena, she'd already left. If she was even there. But look what I found in the ladies' dressing room." Sophie took the silver bracelet out of her jeans pocket and showed it to her mother.

"What's that?"

"It's Barbara Ann's bracelet. I found it under a bench there."

"Oh, my! It's very pretty. How do you know it's hers?"

"There are these initials on the back, see?"

Maman held the bracelet up to the light and examined it. "My, my, my," she said.

Sophie explained about Auntie Marie-Rose finding out where Barbara Ann was staying. And when she phoned her, Barbara Ann even remembered her from high school in Ottawa. "So do you think Papa could drive us to the hotel this afternoon?" Sophie finished all in one breath.

"Oh, I think after the morning he's had, he'd be too exhausted. Besides, I know he was hoping to spend this afternoon working in his garden. But maybe you could ask Joseph. He wouldn't mind, would he?"

"I'll ask him."

Sophie went out to the garage in the backyard where her brother was tinkering with his motorcycle again. But he wasn't alone. A couple of other guys were bent over his bike, nodding at it. They were both rough-looking with dark t-shirts, ragged jeans and oily cowboy boots. One glanced up at her. He had a package of cigarettes rolled into the sleeve of his t-shirt and he was chewing on a matchstick. He grunted in her direction.

The other fellow was even rougher looking, with long greasy hair, dirty fingernails and a stubbly chin. He had a tattoo of a snake encircling his thick forearm.

Although they looked rough and tough, somehow they weren't as scary as the Satan's Rebels bikers who'd run Joseph's motorcycle off the road a few days ago.

"We're meeting them tonight at the pit," the matchstick guy was telling Joseph. "You should come. They're looking for new recruits. They need as many bikers as they can get for a job they're thinking about."

"So who's the kid?" the other one rumbled in a husky voice.

Joseph looked up. "My sister." Sophie had never heard her brother's voice sounding so gritty before. Was he trying to imitate the other fellow?

Sophie decided to ignore the strangers. "Mom and Dad are back and Dad wants to work in his garden this afternoon," she said. "So could you drive us to the hotel to meet Barbara Ann Scott?"

"Ooh. The famous Barbara Ann Scott!" the matchstick

guy said, smirking around his matchstick. He had a front tooth missing. "Heard she's in town. Hubba-hubba, ding, ding."

"Stuff it, Conrad," Joseph snarled at him. He wiped his hands on an oily rag. "Okay, I guess," he said to Sophie. "When do you want to leave?"

"Right away?"

"Got nothin' to lose." Joseph shrugged. "See you guys later."

"At the pit?" Conrad asked.

"Maybe," Joseph said, pulling the garage door closed and latching it.

The two strangers slouched away down the back lane while Joseph followed Sophie into the house. She could tell by the hint of a smile that maybe he was glad to be going to the hotel.

"Give me five minutes to clean up," he said, heading for the bathroom. When he came out, his hands and face were pink from scrubbing and his dark curly hair was slicked back with hair oil.

"*Bryl-creem, a little dab will do ya,*" Auntie Claudine sang, patting the top of his shiny head. "*Bryl-creem. You look so debonair.*"

Blushing, he ducked away from her and grabbed his coat.

They all piled into the car, Auntie Claudine and Joseph in the front, and Auntie Marie-Rose, Sophie and Zephram in the back.

"I don't know why you're coming along," Sophie said to

her little brother. He was snuggled between her and Auntie Marie-Rose.

"I want to meet the famous skater too," he said.

The trip to downtown New Westminster in the car felt so much faster than to the arena on the motorcycle that morning, Sophie could hardly believe it when Joseph pulled the car up to a tall building and announced, "The Royal Hotel. This is it."

They pushed through heavy glass doors and entered a luxurious lobby with glistening tiles on the floor. In the tall windows were giant plants in giant pots. In fact one plant was an actual tree whose top branches touched the high ceiling. The huge fancy room made Sophie feel small and backwoodsy. She should have at least changed into her Sunday dress and coat with the velvet collar instead of wearing her everyday woolly winter jacket.

Joseph was looking uncomfortable as well. But the fancy hotel didn't seem to bother the aunties at all. They both marched straight up to a long shiny desk, their high-heeled shoes click-clacking on the floor tiles. Auntie Claudine announced in a loud demanding voice, "We're here to see Barbara Ann Scott."

Sophie didn't hear what the man behind the desk said. To her it sounded like, "mumble, mumble, mumble."

"Of course, she's expecting us," Auntie Claudine told the man.

"Mumble, mumble, mumble," he said back.

"Fine," she said. "We'll wait for her in the lobby."

She led them to another part of the room which was filled with dark furniture, velvety sofas and stuffed chairs. Huge lamps perched on shiny tables, each giving off a murky yellow glow onto the thick carpet.

"We can wait for her here," she told them, sitting on one of the big stuffed chairs and crossing her legs. "Sit down. Sit down," she urged Sophie and Joseph. "Don't stand there looking like country bumpkins."

"Are you sure we're allowed to sit here?" Sophie asked in a hushed voice. "It looks way too fancy." She glanced around. No one else was using the elegant furniture.

"Of course," her aunt said. "What do you think it's for?"

Sophie and Joseph sat on the edge of a pale blue sofa, but Zephram climbed right up on one of the overstuffed chairs to sit beside Auntie Marie-Rose. He wriggled in to get comfortable and she smiled down at him, patting his knee.

"We shouldn't have to wait too long," she said.

But they did wait. They waited and waited.

Sophie stared at everyone who wandered through the lobby, wondering, "Is that her? Or is that?" Everyone seemed to be in a hurry. Only a few people glanced their way. Sophie shivered with anticipation. Finally she was going to meet her dream. Barbara Ann Scott. She just hoped that she'd have the courage to speak up and ask for her autograph.

Joseph, perched beside her, cracked his knuckles nervously.

After a while, Auntie Claudine said impatiently, "This is

ridiculous. I'll go and ask what's keeping her." She marched to the desk and returned a few minutes later, shaking her head. "There's no answer in her room, so they said that she must have gone out. That's very strange because we told her we'd be coming to see her."

A plump woman wearing a tight purple jacket bustled into the lobby and stopped at the desk. The man behind the desk pointed to Sophie and her relatives and the woman rushed to them, her hands outstretched.

"I do apologize," she said. Her voice was high and breathless. "Miss Scott is not feeling well today. I even made her skip her practice this morning and she's still resting now. Is there something I can help you with?"

Auntie Claudine turned to her. "And who might you be?"

"I'm Mrs. Bertha Banks, Miss Scott's personal manager and helper," the woman said, tugging at her jacket. "And you are?"

Auntie Claudine told her and introduced the rest of the family.

"And how may I help you?" the woman asked again.

"My niece found a bracelet we think belongs to Barbara Ann and we wanted to return it."

"Oh my! You've found her bracelet. She'll be ever so happy. She's been heartbroken, thinking she'd lost it for good. May I see it?"

Sophie took the bracelet out of her pocket and handed it to the woman. She turned it over in her plump hands and examined it.

"Yes, this is her bracelet. I certainly recognize it. She likes to wear this bracelet all the time. I'm sure she will be most grateful to get it back. Thank you so much for returning it, dear," she said to Sophie. "I will see she gets it right away." She turned to leave.

Sophie saw that Joseph was looking as disappointed as she felt.

Gathering up all her courage, she cleared her throat and said, "Wait. We . . . we came all the way into town. Couldn't we at least meet Barbara Ann? And, and I would really like to give her the bracelet myself."

The woman turned back. "As I said, she's resting at the moment. These tours can be most exhausting for the poor dear, and with that sore throat, I insisted that Miss Scott get a proper rest."

"Could we, maybe come back in an hour or so after her rest and see her then?" Sophie persisted. Her heart was pounding. She forced herself to speak up.

"We have so many things to organize for the show. It opens tomorrow night, you know. And we're having a major problem at the moment that we are trying to sort out . . ."

Auntie Marie-Rose said, "I don't understand. We called Barbara Ann earlier today and she remembered me from high school. She said she could see us this afternoon. She's expecting us."

"Oh! You're her little school friend! Why didn't you say so? Of course, she's expecting you. I'll tell her you've arrived, and I'm sure she'll be right down. I try to monitor all her visitors, you know. Sometimes it just gets to be too much for her. Also, you can never be too careful in this day and age."

"And the bracelet?" Auntie Claudine asked, holding out her hand.

"Oh, the bracelet. Of course, you must give it to her yourself." She smiled, and after returning the bracelet to Sophie, she hurried away.

Sophie stashed the bracelet back in her jacket pocket.

A few minutes later a beautiful young woman with long blond hair rushed through the lobby towards them.

Sophie's heart leaped.

"Marie-Rose Peltier!" the woman said in a breathy musical voice. "I'm so sorry to keep you waiting so long. Oh, my! You haven't changed a bit. Not one bit. I'd know you anywhere."

Auntie Marie-Rose leapt up and hugged the woman. "Barbara Ann! So lovely to see you after all these years. I wasn't sure you would remember me."

"How could I forget you," the woman said. "I remember you singing at our graduation. I always thought you sounded like an angel."

Auntie Marie-Rose smiled and said, "I'd like you to meet my nephews and niece. And my cousin too. They're all dying to meet you." She introduced them and Barbara Ann Scott shook everyone's hand, even Zephram's. She shook

Sophie's hand last. Sophie felt her face flush with shyness but she smiled up at her. She was so excited, she felt she was about to pass out.

"And you're the one who found my bracelet at the arena," Barbara Ann said, smiling back at her. She had perfect, shiny white teeth.

Sophie's heart was beating hard with excitement as she fished in her jacket pocket. She drew out the bracelet again and gave it to her.

"Oh, thank you so much, Sophie," Barbara Ann said. "This bracelet is really special to me because it was a gift from my parents for my twenty-first birthday. I'm ever so grateful. I always wear it when I skate. It brings me good luck." She tried to put the bracelet on but she started coughing and had to reach into her pocket for a handkerchief.

"I think the clasp might be broken," Sophie told her.

"You're right. I must have that fixed. Now, I'd like to give you some tickets so you and your family can all come to our opening show tomorrow night as my guests. Your aunt said there are nine of you altogether, so here are the tickets." She gave Sophie a thick envelope.

"Oh, thank you!" Sophie held the envelope to her chest, her heart beating hard. "Thank you so much."

"No, thank *you*, Sophie." The beautiful young woman stared down at her with twinkling blue eyes. "I'm just so happy you found my bracelet."

Sophie cleared her throat. She was so flustered that she

couldn't think of anything else to say. She shoved her hand into her other pocket nervously and her fingers touched her autograph book. She drew it out, and cleared her throat again. "I'd sure love to have your autograph, if . . . if I could?" she said.

"Oh my! Certainly. I'd be more than happy to give it to you." Barbara Ann smiled at Sophie again and took the autograph book. "I think I even have a fountain pen in my purse." She opened a small white leather purse and found an elegant blue fountain pen. "I know just what to write," she said. "This is the best advice I can give anyone, but especially someone your age."

The famous skater sat down on a chair near a small table and pulled the cap off the pen. She flipped open the autograph book and wrote in it quickly, then signed it with a flourish. She blew on the ink to dry it, then handed the autograph book back to Sophie who read out loud what Barbara Ann Scott had written:

> *Those edges and turns teach control and*
> *discipline, just like finger exercises on the*
> *piano. To Sophie LaGrange, gratefully,*
> *Barbara Ann Scott*

And she had dated it, *September 8, 1951.*

"Oh, thank you," Sophie stammered again, holding the autograph book to her chest. "I'll treasure this forever."

Barbara Ann smiled at her again. "Is there anything else

I can do for you to show you my gratitude?"

"Um, yes." Sophie gathered up her courage again. "Um, is there any chance of meeting one of the other skaters?"

"Someone in particular?"

"Well, there was a skater I saw practising alone early this morning at the arena. He, he was wearing a dark sweater and pants and had long dark hair?"

"You must mean Ricardo. He's my partner in some of the dance numbers. Yes, certainly. I could introduce you to him. Maybe tomorrow night at the arena after the show?" Barbara Ann laughed as though it were a joke. Then she coughed into her handkerchief again.

Ricardo, sighed Sophie. She'd never in her life heard such a romantic name. It certainly suited that vision she'd seen on the ice. And now she was actually going to meet him . . .

"Ricardo?" Auntie Marie-Rose asked, suddenly very still. "Not Ricardo Montaine. From high school?"

"Oh, I see that you remember him," Barbara Ann said.

Auntie Marie-Rose blushed. Before she had a chance to say anything else, a tall man wearing wire-rimmed glasses hurried into the lobby, and when he saw Barbara Ann, he rushed over, visibly upset. "There you are. I just can't believe it!" he said, tearing at his thick blond hair. "I just don't know what we're going to do." He took off his glasses and rubbed them on his sweater.

"Oh, Mr. Parfait," Barbara Ann said. "I'd like you to meet a school friend of mine. She's the one I was telling you sang at our graduation and had the most beautiful voice."

"Oh, no." Auntie Marie-Rose shook her head in protest. "Not really."

"Ah!" the manager said, his face wreathed in sudden smiles. "The marvellous singer is here! Right here in the city! So far from Ottawa! Why, that's most extraordinary! And such a beauty as well!" He gallantly bowed to her.

Auntie Marie-Rose raised her eyebrows and gave him a little smile.

"Marie-Rose is here visiting relatives," Barbara Ann told him.

"Do you know what? I've just had an idea. A marvellous idea! My dear," he said, holding Auntie Marie-Rose's hand in both of his, and staring at her above his glasses. "Barbara Ann has told me about your wonderful singing and I wonder if you'd consider singing tomorrow night at our show. Our regular singer can't make it, you see. She's had a family emergency so she had to leave town, and now we can't reach her. She was supposed to organize an organist to accompany her as well, but it seems she hasn't. And here we are, the day before our big opening show, and we have no music. Oh, I just don't know what we're going to do!"

Auntie Marie-Rose's eyes widened. "Sing for the Hollywood Ice Review show? Oh, my! I've never done anything like that before. Especially unaccompanied."

"But Maman could play the organ for you," Sophie said, forgetting about being shy. "She plays for the singers at church all the time. And I could turn the pages for her. I'm pretty good at that."

Auntie Marie-Rose said, "That's true. Alma is a wonderful organist. But what kind of music would it be?"

"It's all well-known music like "The Skater's Waltz" and "The Blue Danube Waltz," and some popular show tunes like "Singing in the Rain" and "Somewhere Over the Rainbow.""

"Oh, we know all those, don't we, Sophie?" Auntie Marie-Rose said.

Sophie nodded.

"The little girl sings as well?"

"Oh, yes," Auntie Claudine said. "She's a very good singer."

"No, no," Sophie protested. Turning the pages of her mother's music book was one thing. Singing in front of a huge audience was something completely different.

"Hmm," the tall manager said. "Maybe we could hear a little song?"

"You mean, here? Right now?" Sophie squeaked. She couldn't believe that she was being asked to sing there, right in front of everyone.

"Sure. No time like the present for a little audition. Come on over to the piano and we'll see how it goes." He ushered them to a shiny black piano sitting in a corner of the lobby. "Now, what will it be? How about "Good Night, Irene?" We use it for our closing number. You know that one?"

"Um, yes," Sophie said, "but I could never . . .""

Before she could protest, the man sat down and played some chords and Auntie Marie-Rose started to sing. *"Last Saturday night . . ."*

She nudged Sophie and nodded for her to join in. Sophie shook her head, but her aunt nudged her again. She had no choice. She cleared her throat and started to sing, quietly at first, then a little louder. Toward the end, she worked her voice to harmonize with her aunt's as they so often did in their family sing-songs. *"I'll see you in my dreams . . ."*

Barbara Ann and Auntie Claudine sat on a sofa in front of the piano, smiling and nodding. Zephram cuddled up into Auntie Claudine's side between them.

Joseph sat across from them and kept glancing at Barbara Ann. Sophie could tell he was trying hard not to stare openly at her. He was smitten with her.

The man played a final chord on the piano with a flourish while the others clapped.

"Good!" the man said. "You two sound good enough to me. In fact, you sound bloody marvellous. Be there at the arena for a dress rehearsal by five thirty tomorrow evening, with your accompanist, and you've got yourselves a job. We'll pay you the usual rate. Wait here for a minute while I get the sheet music from my room and you can all look it over for tomorrow night." He left, galloping across the lobby on his long legs.

Auntie Marie-Rose smiled down at Sophie and hugged her. "Do you think your mother will go for it?"

"Sure hope so." And she did hope her mom would go for it, although it would mean that she, Sophie, would have to sing in front of hundreds of people. She'd have to call upon all her Star Girl courage to do that.

"Your singing was so lovely." Barbara Ann smiled at her and Auntie Marie-Rose. "Just lovely. You two sound much better than our regular singer."

18

Recruiting for the Satan's Rebels

"WHAT? THEY WANT me to play the organ at Queen's Park Arena for the Hollywood Ice Review? And they'll pay how much?" Maman looked as if she couldn't believe her ears when they got home and told her what had happened.

When Auntie Marie-Rose told her how much they would all be paid, and they'd get to see the ice show as well, Maman said, "But what if I don't know the music?"

"Look," Auntie Marie-Rose said, opening the file of sheet music, "it's all popular tunes I'm sure you've played a hundred times before."

Maman flipped through the sheets. She smiled. "You're

right. It sounds like fun. And you'll be singing as well, Sophie?"

Sophie nodded. But her heart was pounding. It was one thing singing with her family, or even in front of a few friends as she'd done at summer camp, but singing at Queen's Park Arena in front of hundreds, maybe even thousands of people? That was quite a different matter.

Maman sat at the piano. She opened the first song and started to play. Auntie Marie-Rose peered over her shoulder and sang, *"When all the world . . ."* She motioned for Sophie to join in at the chorus. *"Somewhere over the rainbow . . ."* they sang together. They sang one song after another. There wasn't one tune Sophie didn't recognize. There were a couple where she didn't know all the words, but she was able to read them over her mother's shoulder.

They practised the tunes after supper until bedtime.

The next morning was Sunday, so everyone had to go to church. Sophie liked to go with Papa to the early eight o'clock service to get it over with. Her two oldest brothers, Joseph and Henri, usually attended early mass as well and served as altar boys.

"Come on. Let's go," Papa called upstairs to the boys' room.

"Coming," Henri answered.

A few minutes later he was downstairs, dressed in his Sunday sweater and pants.

"Where's Joseph?" Papa asked.

"He said he'd come later on his motorcycle."

"You know Father Meunier likes the altar boys to get there early."

Henri shrugged.

Papa puffed impatiently. "Let's go then."

When they got to the church, Sophie wondered if Joseph would arrive on time to serve at the altar. He didn't. She saw him slip into a back pew just as the service was beginning.

Papa glanced back at him. Was he annoyed or disappointed? Sophie couldn't tell.

When they arrived back home, Maman and the aunties were in a flurry of getting ready with fancy hats and perfumed gloves to go to High Mass. Zephram was dressed in his new sailor suit and he waited by the front porch, bouncing his shiny red ball to Arthur who was also going to High Mass.

"Now, don't you boys get dirty," Maman called out to them.

After the three women and the boys had left for the church service, Sophie helped Papa get Sunday dinner ready. Sunday dinner was his specialty, pot-roast with potatoes and lots of his garden vegetables. There was a chocolate cake with yummy chocolate icing for dessert that Auntie Claudine had made the evening before.

Sophie set the table in the kitchen, thinking about the performance for the Hollywood Ice Review at Queen's Park Arena that night. Her stomach grumbled and fluttered nervously. All those people! The bleachers would be packed full of people. Strangers. What if she lost her voice in front of everyone? Or screeched? Well then, Auntie Marie-Rose would have to sing the songs all by herself. But it would all be just so embarrassing.

Sunday dinner was ready when Maman and the aunties returned home after mass. They hung up their coats and hats and fluffed up their hair as they came into the kitchen.

"Smells absolutely delicious, André," Auntie Claudine said. "Wish I could find a man who's such a good cook."

"Come and taste it before you say things like that," Papa said, grinning. "Sophie, could you call the boys?"

Sophie had heard Joseph's motorcycle return from church earlier so she thought he was probably in the garage tinkering away on it as usual. She went out to the backyard and heard the growl of a motorcycle motor. But it wasn't Joseph's. His was sitting in the garage surrounded by tools and oily rags.

Sophie pushed open the back gate and saw two other motorcycles rumbling away down the lane.

The Satan's Rebels gang! she thought.

Joseph was standing at the garage door watching them. He wasn't smiling.

Henri was near the gate and staring the motorcycles as well. He wasn't smiling either. In fact, he was looking really worried. Even scared. He'd taken off his glasses and was polishing them nervously on his shirttail.

The bikers turned their motorcycles in a loop and headed back towards them along the lane, the motors growling threateningly. Both bikers were wearing black jackets.

"What's happening?" Sophie hissed to Henri. "Want me to get Papa?"

"Not yet. I think it's okay." Henri shook his head. "I think Joseph's taking care of it, but it sure is crazy!" he muttered. "They grabbed Joe's aviation helmet off the back of his motorcycle and they ran over it. Look! They're running over it again!"

Sophie saw the wheels of the motorcycles, one after the other, grind the leather helmet into the gravel.

"No! Not his new helmet!" Sophie cried. "They can't do that! Joe! Stop them!"

But her oldest brother just stood there, hands in his pockets, and stared down at his crushed helmet.

Sophie couldn't stand it another minute. She exploded out of the yard and rushed at the lead motorcycle. "You hooligans stop that right this minute!" she yelled, waving her arms at them. "That's my brother's helmet. How dare you run over it!"

The motorcycle skidded to an abrupt stop at her feet. The other one had to swerve widely to avoid bashing into it and he almost fell.

The bikers both stared at Sophie, frowning. "What's it to you, kid?" the lead driver asked her, gruffly.

"That's my brother's brand new helmet you just ran

over," she yelled at him. "You have no right to do that. That's private property."

"What's this crazy pipsqueak doing, Joe?" he said, jerking his thumb in Sophie's direction. "D'ya know her?"

Joseph came out to the lane. "Told you before. She's my sister."

The biker laughed a harsh laugh. "A regular spitfire, that one is." When he grinned at Sophie, she saw he had a front tooth missing. Now she recognized him. He was the same fellow she had seen with Joseph in the lane the day before. He'd called him Conrad.

"What's going on here?" Sophie asked, staring from the biker to her brother.

Joseph waved her back. "It's really okay, Soph. No big deal. I'm taking care of it."

Sophie backed away to the fence. All of a sudden, she felt foolish. She hadn't realized Joseph knew these guys. Maybe they were even his friends. Although they surely weren't acting very friendly.

The biker reached over and grabbed Joseph's shirt sleeve. "Step one to becoming a member of Satan's Rebels," he growled in Joseph's face.

Sophie tensed her muscles, ready to leap on the ruffian's back and pound his head with her fists if he hurt her brother. Friend or no friend.

The biker spat at Joseph's feet. "Your hat's been driven over twice," he continued. "That's the invitation. Step two is show up at the gravel pit in the park tonight for the initiation. That's what we did last night so now Jake and me, we're officially associate members."

"Now why would I do that?" Joseph asked.

"Lucifer, he's the chief, says they want every biker in town in their society," Conrad said. "It's going to be the biggest motorcycle club around. Every new member can buy one of these leather jackets at a real low price." Conrad turned around so they could see "Satan's Rebels" spelled out in shiny star-shaped nail studs on the back of his jacket. The other biker had one the same.

"Neat," Joseph said.

"So you better show up if you know what's good for you. You got that?" The biker punched Joseph's shoulder lightly, then tipped his hat. It was a ragged officer's hat with a battered visor that looked as if it had been run over a few times as well. He glared at Sophie and Henri, revved up his motor and sped away. The other biker followed him and raised his fist at Joseph as his bike spewed up gravel in their faces.

Sophie wiped the dust from her face and they watched the bikers leave, then Joseph ambled down the lane to retrieve his aviation helmet. When he picked it up, the strap hung down like the tail of a dead squirrel.

"So what's that all about?" Sophie asked him.

"Looks like they're recruiting for Satan's Rebels," he said, trying to brush the dirt off his helmet.

"Satan's Rebels! Are we joining them?" Henri asked, his

eyes huge behind his glasses. "They're a gang, aren't they? A real motorcycle gang? A new one. They're moving up here from the States. I heard about them at school. I heard they're doing all kinds of nasty stuff."

"Don't know yet if we'll be joining any gang." Joseph shrugged. "Maybe."

"Oh, Joe. You shouldn't," Sophie said. "Those guys look really tough. Almost as tough as those other Satan's Rebels bikers who ran us off the road last week."

"What bikers?" Henri asked. "You didn't tell me some guys from the Satan's Rebels ran you off the road."

"No big deal." Joseph shrugged. "We just sort of ran into them. And about those two bikers, Conrad and his friend, Jake? It's okay. I know them from working down at the mill. Conrad used to be on my hockey team. In fact he's a terrific skater. They're really not as bad as they look."

He pulled the bedraggled helmet onto his head and, narrowing his eyes, he glared at Sophie.

Now her brother looked as tough as the bikers.

19

Mary Ellen

AFTER DINNER, MAMAN said, "How about a quick rehearsal for the show tonight?"

Sophie grinned. Practising the songs meant she'd get out of doing the dishes, even though it was her turn to dry. She'd already cleared the table, which was Joseph's job, since she'd promised to do all his chores for the next month for taking her to Queen's Park Arena the day before.

"Not fair," Arthur complained. "I dried last night."

"Sophie will take your place another time," Maman said. "Now don't be so inflexible, Arthur."

There were just eight songs in the show and the rest of

the numbers were for the organ alone. After they'd practised the songs a few times, Maman said to Auntie Marie-Rose and Sophie, "That sounded very good to me. Now, I think you should both rest your voices until tonight."

Sophie slipped out the front door in case Arthur wasn't finished drying the dishes yet. She snuck around the side of the house to the backyard to ride on the swing hanging from a high branch in the cherry tree. It was a clear, sunny afternoon, and the leaves were starting to turn yellow and drift down from the tall tree.

Joseph was out in the garage. She peered over the gate to see if he was alone. He was, so she asked him if he could give her a ride on his motorcycle.

"Where do you want to go?" he asked.

"Remember my friend, Mary Ellen?"

"Your little friend I gave a ride home to a couple days ago?"

"Yes. Could you take me to her place? You remember where she lives, right?"

"Sure I remember. White house up on Austin. But why? What's up?"

"I don't know where she lives and I don't have her phone number, but I'd like to give her a couple of tickets for the Hollywood Ice Review tonight because Mom and Auntie Marie-Rose and I won't need our tickets since we're doing the music. I know Mary Ellen would really like to see the show too."

"Okay," he said. "I guess. Don't have anything better to do."

"Great! I'll just get the tickets and I'll be right back."

Sophie crouched behind her brother's broad back as they blasted up Blue Mountain Road on his motorcycle. There weren't many cars on the road, just a few people out taking a Sunday afternoon drive.

As they were passing the smelly mink farm cages hidden behind some bushes, Sophie heard the throb of a loud motor behind them. She glanced back over her shoulder. Through the dust and exhaust of Joe's motorcycle, she saw at least one other motorcycle, if not two or three. The motorcycles were gaining on them. Soon they came alongside. Sophie's heart raced and she felt Joseph tense the muscles in his shoulders as he steered his bike away from them to the road's edge.

"Watch out, Joe!" Sophie squealed. "They'll bash into us!"

As the motorcycles cut them off, Joseph was forced to turn his bike sharply. It bounced through the long grass and lurched down into the ditch. Sophie jerked up her feet so they wouldn't be crushed by the ditch's sides.

The bike stalled abruptly and she was thrown forward, bashing her face against Joseph's back. Her chin stung painfully.

The other motorcycles skidded to a stop above them. There were four bikers, all wearing dark sunglasses and dressed identically in jeans, black leather jackets and German officers' hats with shiny visors. They towered over Joseph and Sophie from their massive black bikes up on the bank.

"What'd you do that for?" Joseph demanded in a voice loud enough to be heard over the growling motors.

"Humph," the lead biker grunted. He shoved a lock of hair away from his eyes and stared hard down at them. "Heard you been talkin' to those new recruits. Conrad and his pal. Heard your name's Joe." He was chewing the end of a small cigar.

"So?" Joseph said.

Sophie thought he was the same biker that had chased her down the lane. What if he recognized her and accused her of spying? She pulled her collar up over her sore chin to her nose and tried to keep out of his sight.

"They call me Lucifer," the biker said.

Joseph nodded.

"Bit of advice, Joe," the biker said out of the corner of his mouth. "You want to show up at the pit tonight, see. We got a job and we need every biker in town there."

"So I hear," Joseph said.

The biker leaned his motorcycle over. Now his face was so close, Sophie could see a bit of moustache growing on his upper lip and smell the cigar smoke. "You wanna join our biker society, see? If you don't show up tonight, we got ways of making life not so pleasant for you, see?"

Joseph didn't say anything.

"Say something," Sophie hissed in Joseph's ear.

But Joseph's lips were tightly closed.

Sophie had to force herself to remain silent and not yell at the mean biker herself. If Joseph wasn't talking, he must have a good reason.

"You got that, Joe?" the biker said. "Pit in the park. Sundown tonight. Be there." He took a drag on his cigar and blew smoke into Joseph's face.

Sophie held her breath. What was he going to do next? Her muscles were tensed. She'd leap up and fight this bully if she had to. Pound his head. Pull his hair. Scratch his eyes out. Fight them all. Fight them to the bitter end. Her hero Star Girl wouldn't sit back and watch her brother get beat up without fighting back.

Finally Joseph grunted. "Okay," he muttered. "Okay."

The biker smiled around his cigar. "Nice bike, that English job. Bit light though. When you're in, we could give you a lead on a real nice bike. A hog like this, maybe." He patted the front of his motorcycle.

"Harley Davidson," Sophie read the letters on the motorcycle in front of the biker's knees.

He nodded to the other bikers. Their motors growled and they blasted off, spraying out gravel and smoky exhaust.

Joseph coughed then wiped his nose on the back of his hand and took a deep breath. "You okay?" he asked her when the throb of motors had died down.

"Yes. You?" Sophie rubbed her stinging eyes on her sleeve.

"Yeah, I guess," he said, climbing off the bike.

"So what's that all about?" she asked him, climbing off as well.

He shook his head. "Looks like they're recruiting new members for the Satan's Rebels gang."

"They're really bad, aren't they? Like gangsters, or something?"

"Maybe."

"Papa read an article in the paper about them. He called them hooligans. You'd never join their gang, would you?" Sophie couldn't imagine her nice, kind, funny brother ever belonging to a gang of hooligans who had a reputation as bad as the Satan's Rebels.

"Don't know, kiddo." He cleared his throat. "I just don't know. Want to give me a hand pushing the bike out of the ditch?"

He pulled his goggles back down over his eyes, making his face hard to read.

Was he scared? Was he mad?

Or was he excited?

Mary Ellen was alone, playing hopscotch on the sidewalk when Joseph stopped the motorcycle in front of her house. It was a small white house behind a freshly painted white picket fence. Sophie climbed off the motorcycle and opened the gate.

"Hi, Mary Ellen," she said.

"Hi-ya, Sophie. What's up?" she asked. She glanced shyly in Joseph's direction.

"How'd you like to go to the Hollywood Ice Review tonight? I've got a couple of extra tickets."

"Oh, I'd love to. But I already asked my ma, and she said we could never afford such a luxury."

"The tickets are free." Sophie pulled them out of her pocket.

"Free? What's the catch?"

"It's a really long story. I'll tell you about it tomorrow at school. D'you want them or not?"

"Course I want them. Are you going too?"

"Yes." Sophie nodded. She didn't want to tell Mary Ellen about having to sing. The manager had told them the singers and the organist would have their own little box and they wouldn't be visible to the audience. No one would even know who it was making the music. So if she squawked, no one would know who to blame.

"Just a minute. I'll ask my ma if we can go."

Mary Ellen was back in seconds, her freckled face grinning. "She said yes! Oh, that's so great. She said yes!" She grabbed Sophie's arm and danced around chanting, "We're going to see Barbara Ann Scott!"

"See you tonight then," Sophie said.

"Gosh! Thanks a lot, Sophie." Mary Ellen followed her to the gate and glanced shyly up at Joseph again and sighed.

Sophie grinned to herself. Now she got it. Her oldest brother had a not-so-secret admirer.

20
Another Catastrophe

PAPA DROVE MAMAN, Auntie Marie-Rose and Sophie to the arena early so they would have time to practise the tunes with the organ before the ice show.

Sophie, dressed in her Sunday best, sat in the back seat of Papa's car with Auntie Marie-Rose, who was strangely silent. She stared out the car window, twisting her hanky and biting her lower lip. She couldn't be nervous about singing. She'd sung a lot in public and the songs they had tonight were all easy and she knew them well. Sophie wondered what else could be bothering her, but she couldn't think of the words to ask her.

Papa let them off near the main front entrance of the arena.

"See you later, dear." Maman kissed him goodbye. "Wish us luck now."

He would return later with Auntie Claudine, Zephram and Arthur in the car. Henri would follow with Joseph on Joseph's motorcycle. If Joseph decided to come. If they didn't go to the gravel pit for the Satan's Rebels' initiation.

Sophie almost told Maman about the motorcycle gang, but she knew Joseph would have been so mad at her, sticking her nose into his business. But what about that newspaper article Papa had read? It sure sounded as if joining that gang was not at all a good idea. If Joseph did join, Sophie knew that Henri would join as well. Pretty well whatever Joseph did, Henri was always right behind. Would she want her brothers to be part of a bunch of such rough bikers? It looked to her as if the Satan's Rebels spelled nothing but trouble.

She peered around the parking lot as she led the way to the big entrance doors. A few cars were already parked but no motorcycles.

The doors were locked.

"The show doesn't start until 7:30. Doors open at 6:30," a man dressed in a dark blue uniform told them.

"We're the musicians," Maman informed him.

"Oh! In that case, madam, follow me." He shook out a clump of keys from his belt and unlocked the doors. They

followed him inside, past the box office, and across the corridor to a long dimly lit hallway. A steep stairway led up to
a small door. "This is where the organ and microphones are,"
he told them, opening the door. "We call it the Organ Box."

It was a small room, way smaller than their living room.
There was just enough room for the four of them to crowd
in together with the organ and its bench, a chair and two
silver-coloured microphones. Sophie's heart was beating so
fast with excitement, she felt all fluttery. Even her knees felt
weak. One good thing, she reminded herself, at least the
audience wouldn't be able to see them from the bleachers.

The man fiddled with the organ, turning it on. "I'll leave
you to try out the equipment," he told them and left, closing the door behind him.

For a minute the small room was strangely silent. The
only sound was the organ humming softly, warming up, and
Maman flipping through the folder of sheet music. On one
side of the room was a big opening, like a window with no
glass. Through it, Sophie had a good view of most of the ice
below.

"We'll be able to see the whole show from here," she said,
peering down at the rink. It was in darkness at the moment.
The only light was the light coming from their little room.
It shone dimly out over a few rows of bleachers and onto
the edge of the ice.

"This organ is quite different from the wheezy old one I
play at the church," Maman said. "I wonder what all these

knobs are for." She sat down on the bench and started fiddling with them.

Sophie realized that she had to use the washroom, desperately. She should have gone before they left home, but the one bathroom in the house had been busy with Maman and Auntie Marie-Rose primping and getting ready for the evening.

"I have to go to the washroom," she told Maman.

"Oh, dear." Maman propped the sheet music on the organ and played a couple of chords. "I want to try out the organ to see how it works before the show. Maybe Marie-Rose could take you to find a washroom."

"It's okay. I can find a washroom myself. There must be one close by."

Sophie wandered back along the dim hallway and into the main corridor. There wasn't anyone there to ask for directions. She didn't know which way to go. Then she heard some people coming down the corridor. It was a group of young women.

"Excuse me," she said to them. "Could you please tell me where there's a washroom?"

"Sure thing," one of them said. "You can use the one in the dressing room. Just follow us." She was a tall woman who moved easily on long legs. She looked familiar.

"Say, aren't you Sally?" Sophie asked her. "Um, Sally Steele?"

"Yes. Have we met?"

"A few days ago. My friend and I met you in the bleachers. You gave me your autograph. Remember?"

"Oh, right! The two kids playing hooky." She grinned down at Sophie.

"We weren't playing hooky. Not really."

"Tell that to the judge," Sally laughed. "Hey, here's the dressing room. The toilets are in through that door."

"Thanks." Sophie thought it was the same dressing room where she'd found the bracelet, but today it was brightly lit. Several young women were doing their hair and putting on makeup in front of long mirrors. Sophie hurried through it to the toilets. When she came out, sitting there on a bench, tying up her skates, was Barbara Ann Scott!

Sophie was about to say hello to her when there was a loud knock on the door.

"Everybody decent?" a man's voice called out.

Sally peered around. No one was undressed so she said, "Sure, Mr. Parfait. Come on in."

The tall manager with glasses and unruly hair bustled in, all in a flutter. He didn't even notice Sophie standing there.

"More major problems, I'm afraid," he told the skaters.

"Oh no! This show must be jinxed," Sally said. "What's happened now?"

"It's that darn Ricardo Montaine. He's gone. And this time it looks as if he's gone for good."

At the mention of his name, Sophie's heart skipped a beat. Her dark Ice Phantom.

"Gone?" another skater said. "What are you talking about?"

"I looked in his room at the hotel, and all his stuff's gone too. The man at the desk said he'd checked out."

"Why, he can't do that! Not on the very day of our opening show."

"He was threatening to leave if I didn't double his salary and make him the star of the show. But I never thought he'd actually do it. Apparently, he's gone to join the New York Ice Review. They made him such a good offer he couldn't refuse, so he hopped the night train to go east. I just don't know what we'll do tonight." He ran his fingers through his thick hair until it stood up like a rooster's comb. "So here's the deal. I was thinking about taking one of the young men from the chorus to be your partner, Barbara Ann. Which one do you think would fit in the best?"

"Probably Billy Joel," one of the skaters said. "I know he's wanted to dance the lead for months."

"But you can't take Billy from the chorus," Sally said. "He's my partner and we'd be one fellow short. That would ruin our routines, especially our big opening number."

"Yes," piped up another skater. "Cutting out one of our fellows would really throw us off. Can't you find another male skater somewhere?"

Barbara Ann shook her head. Her forehead was creased with worry.

"Find another skater at this late date?" the manager said.

"Except for those kids from the local skating club who are in that "Teddy Bears' Picnic" number, "I don't know anyone around this town. Where can I find a male skater at an hour's notice?" His eyes fell on Sophie. "Say, you're the kid whose mother's playing the organ for us tonight, right? What are you doing here?"

"She just came to use the washroom," one of the skaters told him.

"You don't happen to have a good male ice skater up your sleeve, do you?" The manager grinned down at Sophie.

"Um, well actually, I think my brother Joseph's a really good skater. He's been skating forever. He took figure skating lessons for years when we lived in Montreal."

"You're kidding, right?"

"No, really." Sophie nodded, forgetting about being shy. "And he plays hockey for the New Westminster Royals. He's their fastest skater. And they win a lot of games. They might even get to go to the Olympics in a few years."

Barbara Ann smiled at her. "I think I met him yesterday," she said. "Isn't he the tall handsome young man that drove you to the hotel when you came to return my bracelet?" She held out her arm to show it shining there.

Sophie smiled at the fact that Barbara Ann was calling Joseph tall and handsome. She wished he were here to hear it. "Yes," she said. "That's my brother Joseph. I'm not sure if he is coming to the show tonight, or not." She suddenly remembered the two rough bikers in the lane, and them telling

Joe to go to the gravel pit for the motorcycle gang meeting tonight. And the other Satan's Rebels members who'd stopped them that afternoon. "We'd better telephone him right now. If you tell him he's needed to be part of the show, I think he'd come for sure."

"If he's a good skater, the program shouldn't be any problem for him," said Mr. Parfait. "Just a matter of following the skater in front of him, and holding onto his partner's hand when she offers it."

"That would be me," Sally said. "A lot of it is mirror skating and I could talk him through the spins and jumps. No problem. I could show him a couple of tricky bits before the show starts if he gets here soon enough."

"Looks like our best bet," the manager said. "Come on, kid. Let's go find a telephone. The show must go on." He raised his fist into the air.

Sophie trotted after Mr. Parfait as he strode to the box office which was a tiny room near the entrance. It was cluttered with papers and folders all over the desk and shelves.

"Where's that telephone anyway?" the manager growled, shifting the piles of papers around. "Aha!" He found it under a stack of files and handed it to Sophie.

Sophie lifted the receiver and asked the operator for Coquitlam 703. The telephone rang and rang.

The operator came back on and said, "I'm sorry. There's no answer."

"Thanks," Sophie said and hung up. "He must have already left," she said to Mr. Parfait, imagining her brother on his way to the gravel pit.

"Oh no! Now what?" Mr. Parfait looked desperate. "One skater short will totally mess up the routines. I'll have to go and break the news to the skaters. I just don't know what we're going to do."

He strode away back to the dressing rooms.

21

Rumble

SOPHIE KNEW NOW where Joseph was heading.

She dashed to the entrance doors. If only she could get there on time. Once outside, she hurried along the side of the big building. Then she darted into the bushes at the back where she and Mary Ellen had found a trail a few days ago. The setting sun cast purple shadows in front of her. She knew she was heading in the right direction because soon she heard the deep growl of motorcycle motors. So the club was already meeting.

She burst out of the woods into the clearing. There was a smoky bonfire beside a mound of gravel and several motorcycles were gathered around it. Most of the motorcycles held two riders. Sophie was surprised that some of them were girls wearing plenty of lipstick and eye shadow and had cigarettes hanging out of their mouths.

In the dim light, no one noticed her. She scanned the crowd. Her brothers weren't there. She crept closer to a bunch of bikers.

"So when they're done the show, they'll come out that side door. That's when we grab her, load her into the back of the car we got waiting, then hightail it out of there."

"But what if she screams?"

"That's where you guys come in. At the signal, which will be turning on the car headlights, you all start rolling into the parking lot, revving up your motors real loud. That will cause a distraction and no one will hear her."

"How will you know which one's her?"

"We'll know her all right. She's the blond one."

"I don't know," one biker was shaking his head. Sophie thought maybe it was Conrad. "She might have a body guard. Sounds awful risky to me."

"'Course you'd say that, dink. Cause you're a new recruit . . .'"

"Who you calling a dink?" Conrad growled, grabbing the other biker's jacket.

"Look, guys," another biker stepped between them and shoved them apart. "We gotta stick together on this job. Tonight might be our last chance to grab the dame. They won't be expecting it, so we got the element of surprise, see. We just grab her, stuff her into the back seat of the car, and beat it. They'll be willing to pay big bucks to get their fancy star back to finish the show here. We get the dough, pronto. They get the dame back. Nothing to it. Nobody gets hurt. All in a night's work."

Sophie gasped. Barbara Ann! They were planning to kidnap Barbara Ann! She stepped back and stumbled over a rock.

A biker reeled around and stared right at her. He lurched out of the crowd and faced her. "So if it isn't little Miss Nosey Snoop," he spat in her face.

He was the tall biker with long black hair. Lucifer. "Spying on us again, huh?"

Sophie backed away. "No, no . . ."

Before she could escape, he grabbed her sleeve. "I'll teach you to . . ."

Over his shoulder Sophie saw another bike arriving along the lane. It was Joseph! And Henri!

"Joe!" she yelled in her loudest voice, waving her arm at him. "Joe! Henri!"

Henri's head turned. His glasses glinted at her. He'd seen her. She was sure of it. Now he was telling Joseph. Joseph swerved the bike and aimed it at her and the biker. He roared forward and skidded to a stop inches from them.

"Get your hands off that kid," Joseph growled as he got off the bike.

Sophie had never heard him use such a rough voice before.

"Yeah? What's it to you?" Lucifer snarled.

Joseph grabbed Lucifer's collar and almost ripped it off. The biker let go of Sophie.

She was going to make tracks out of there, but they were suddenly surrounded by a bunch of other bikers.

"Hop on the back, Soph," Joseph muttered. "Now!"

Henri leaned forward and she leapt on the motorcycle behind him on the narrow luggage rack. There wasn't much room.

Henri clasped her knees and she wrapped her arms around his waist.

Before the gang members had time to stop them, Joseph revved up the motor and they blasted through the crowd and out of the gravel pit.

The lane had lots of puddles and the bike bounced into every one, splashing muddy water onto Sophie's legs. But she clung to Henri's back like a suction cup from a dart gun until they reached the parking lot in front of the arena.

A lot of people were there, so Sophie thought the bikers wouldn't follow them to such a public place.

Joseph stopped the motorcycle and she slid off the back.

She was panting, but she had so much to tell her brothers. She grabbed the motorcycle's handlebars and swallowed hard. "Joe! They need you. In there," she shouted to be heard above its motor. "It's important. One of the guys dropped out of the show. And they need you."

"What?"

"I was coming to tell you that at the gravel pit. And, and, something else. I heard those guys are planning to kidnap someone."

"What are you talking about?"

"Really. And I think that someone's Barbara Ann! We got to do something!"

Henri's mouth dropped open in surprise.

"You sure, Soph?" Joseph stared at her with huge eyes.

Sophie nodded frantically. "Tonight. They're going to grab her tonight. After the show."

"Let's get going then," Joseph said. He parked his bike and they rushed to the arena.

By now the entrance doors were open and an excited crowd was lining up, tickets in hand.

Ignoring the crowd's angry stares, Sophie and her brothers pushed past them and burst into the arena.

"Hey, kids," a man at the entrance called out. "Don't you know there's a line? Where are your tickets?"

"We — we're in the show," Sophie stammered. "I'm singing. And my brothers. They're skating. Remember me from earlier?"

The man scratched his head. "Right," he said. "You came in earlier with the two ladies. Okay, off you go. There's not much time. The show's starting soon." And he hurried forward to direct the customers.

"Okay, Soph," Joseph said, holding her shoulders. "Calm down. Tell us again what's happening."

Sophie took a deep breath. "First, they need you in the show because one of the skaters dropped out."

"What? They want *me* to be in that show? It's been a couple of years since I did any figure skating."

"You can do it, Joe. Mr. Parfait said you'd just have to follow what the guy in front of you does and hold onto your partner's hand when she holds it out. It's Sally Steele and she said she'd talk you through it. She said she could show you a couple of the tricky bits before the show starts."

Joseph hesitated.

"You *have* to help them, Joe. You just *have* to."

"I guess I could give it a shot," he said. "Hope they've got a spare pair of skates, size ten. But what's this about kidnapping Barbara Ann?"

"Those bikers at the gravel pit. They said they're going to grab Barbara Ann on her way out of the arena after the show. They were talking about it a few days ago, but I didn't figure it out until tonight."

"That's crazy," Henri said, shaking his head. "They'd never get away with it."

"They might. They've got a car ready to put her in after they grab her. And there's a whole gang of them to cause a distraction with their motorcycles."

Joseph was shaking his head in disbelief.

"We got to stop them," Sophie said. "We don't have much

time. The show's starting soon. You've got to go to the dressing room, Joe. The show depends on you."

"Is there a phone around here?" Henri said. "I'll call the police."

"Yes, in the office. I'll show you where," Sophie said.

"Just one thing, Soph," Joseph said.

"What?"

"Don't tell Mom about the bikers' plans. She's already worried enough about me riding around on a motorcycle."

Sophie hesitated.

Joseph's dark eyes were begging her.

Finally she nodded. "All right. I won't tell her. But maybe she'll find out anyway."

"As long as she doesn't connect me with them," he said and hurried away while Sophie led Henri to the office. "The phone's in there somewhere. You'll find it." Then she dashed away to the organ box.

"Oh, Sophie!" Auntie Marie-Rose said. "I was about to go and search for you. Whatever happened? Did you get lost?"

"No." Sophie shook her head. She took a deep breath. "You won't believe it! Joseph's going to skate in the show tonight!"

"What?" Maman swung around. "Our Joseph in the show?"

"You know that Ricardo Montaine? Well, he left town by train for New York this afternoon. He's going to be in the New York Ice Review."

"How do you know that?" Auntie Marie-Rose's voice

sounded strangled and her face grew strangely pale.

"That's what the manager, Mr. Parfait, said."

Auntie Marie-Rose turned away. She fished in her pocket and brought out a hanky to blow her nose.

Sophie couldn't figure it out. Why was her aunt so upset?

22

The Show Must Go On

"LADIES AND GENTLEMEN. Boys and girls," the announcer's voice blared over the loudspeakers about half an hour later. Sophie thought it sounded like Mr. Parfait. "Welcome to the one, the only, Hollywood Ice Review, starring the world famous Olympic gold medallist, our own Canada's Sweetheart, Barbara Ann Scott!"

Maman pounded on the organ's keyboard, and out poured loud welcoming music as Barbara Ann Scott skated onto the ice. She was wearing a sparkly yellow costume and she raised her arms and smiled, greeting the crowd.

The crowd clapped and cheered.

The announcer went on. "And as her partner tonight, may I introduce skating sensation, Billy Joel."

Maman played another fanfare as Billy, dressed all in black, skated out to join Barbara Ann.

The crowd clapped and cheered some more.

Then Maman broke into the opening number which was "The Skater's Waltz." A line of other skaters dressed in sparkly costumes streamed onto the ice, joining Barbara Ann and Billy. There, at the end of the line, was Joseph! Sophie recognized him right away. The troupe skated around the rink forming complicated arcs and rings.

Sophie's heart was in her mouth. She hoped beyond hope that Joseph wouldn't trip and fall flat on his face out there in front of all those people.

But he was fine. He really was. He followed the other skaters around the ice, matching his strides with theirs. All those skating lessons he'd taken for years in Montreal were paying off.

Barbara Ann and her partner were gorgeous to watch. Billy followed her like a shadow, holding her hand when she offered it. He wasn't as handsome as the mysterious Ricardo, but Sophie soon forgot about him. Billy was tall and graceful and Barbara Ann was so pretty and sparkly that they made a perfect dream couple.

When "The Skater's Waltz" came to an end, Maman flipped over the pages to "The Night Becomes You." Barbara Ann skated off the ice and Billy followed her while the other skaters skated around in colourful loops and giant figure eights. Sophie couldn't keep her eyes off Joseph at the end of the line. She didn't notice him faltering even once. Whatever the skater in front of him did, he followed perfectly, stride for stride. When the line stopped, he stood by and watched Sally do a camel spin, his hands out, ready to support her, just as all the other male skaters were doing with their partners. Then the partners joined hands, and skated around together.

After Maman played the introduction to the song, she nodded at Sophie and Auntie Marie-Rose, signalling them to start singing.

Auntie Marie-Rose stood at the microphone and sang, "When twilight falls . . ."

Sophie froze. She gulped hard. She couldn't even get her mouth open.

Auntie Marie-Rose motioned to her to come and stand closer to the microphone so Sophie crept beside her and stared out at the ice. She still couldn't force her mouth open. Her heart was pounding so hard, she felt lightheaded.

Auntie Marie-Rose smiled at her and nodded encouragingly. She pointed to the words on the song sheet.

"Come on, Star Girl! You can do it," swirled around in Sophie's head. "You can do it!"

She took a deep breath and somehow she got her mouth open. Then, staring down at her brother swooping around the rink, doing neat crossovers at the corners, she forced herself to start singing along. "No one can even see me," she told herself. And her aunt had such a loud and powerful voice, they probably wouldn't even be able to hear hers.

When Maman started the music for the next song, Auntie Marie-Rose smiled and nodded at Sophie again. She cleared her throat and managed to join in right at the beginning.

If Joseph could go out there and skate in front of hundreds of spectators, she should be able to do a bit of what she knew how to do best: sing the familiar songs and harmonize along with her aunt, her mother accompanying them on the organ.

The more Sophie sang, the easier it became. Eventually she forgot about feeling nervous. She lost count of the songs they sang, one after another.

She thought her aunt's voice sounded really sweet tonight, especially when she sang, *"I'll be seeing you . . ."* Her voice soared up to the rafters. But her dark eyes were shining with unshed tears, and she kept dabbing at them with her hanky. By the end of the song, tears were streaming down her cheeks. Sophie wondered what had upset her so much.

Finally the organ rolled into "Good Night, Irene," the evening's final number.

Barbara Ann and Billy skated out onto the ice both wearing deep red costumes with sparkles all over. Barbara Ann performed the most amazing twirls and whirls and swirls while Billy stood by to support her. They swooped around from one end of the rink to the other. When Barbara Ann leapt up and twirled around a couple of times before landing on the ice to be supported by Billy's outstretched arms, the whole audience erupted into a roar of applause. She did it again. And again. The audience went crazy.

Finally, Barbara Ann and Billy skated to the middle of the rink. They raised their arms and bowed, acknowledging the crowd. The crowd clapped and roared some more, and the couple bowed again as Maman played the last verse and Sophie and her aunt sang, *"I'll see you in my dreams."*

Auntie Marie-Rose's voice faltered. She had become too upset to continue. So Sophie put her mouth close to the microphone and finished the song on her own.

As the song came to an end, Sophie's aunt patted her hand and gave her a wobbly smile. Barbara Ann and Billy skated off the ice but they had to return for several encores with all the other skaters in the troupe, including Joseph, before the clapping and cheering audience would let them go.

Finally, the manager's voice came over the loudspeakers. "Ladies and gentlemen, boys and girls. Thank you so much for coming out to our show tonight. I must tell you that our glorious music tonight was provided by your own local organist, Mrs. Alma LaGrange and her daughter Sophie, and the singing sensation, all the way from Ottawa, Miss Marie-Rose Peltier. Please put your hands together to thank them for a most wonderful musical evening."

The crowd clapped and roared some more.

Then Maman played "God Save the King" and the audience stood, knowing it was the end of the show. They sang the anthem, then trailed out of the bleachers.

"Well!" Maman played the last chord. "That's it. You girls did a wonderful job," she said as she gathered up the sheet music into the folder. She turned around and saw Auntie Marie-Rose dabbing her red eyes and nose. "Now, now, *chérie*," she said, patting her cheek. "Whatever is the matter?"

"Oh, it's nothing," Auntie Marie-Rose sniffed. "Nothing at all. I must be getting a cold or something."

But Sophie knew it must be something more than a cold. Something had happened that had really upset her aunt. What could it be?

Also her mind was filled with what was happening down at the players' entrance. Were Satan's Rebels bikers lying in wait to kidnap Barbara Ann? Or had her brother managed to contact the police? She listened hard but she couldn't hear any sirens. Or any growling motorcycle motors.

23

The Finale

"THAT WAS SPLENDID. Simply splendid!" the manager said, rushing into the tiny organ box. "The music was positively magnificent! How can I ever thank you?" He shook Maman's hand and Sophie's. Then he held Auntie Marie-Rose's hand in his two hands and gazed down at her with delight in his eyes. "Barbara Ann was absolutely right. You really do have the voice of an angel."

"No, not really." Auntie Marie-Rose shook her head. Sophie thought her aunt looked so beautiful, with her pale pink cheeks and dark, glittering eyes. "But thank you. I'm glad it was okay."

"Oh, more than okay. Much more. It was positively marvellous. The best I've ever heard. I would like to ask if you could provide the music for our show for the rest of the week."

"The rest of the week?" Maman said. "Well, it's fine with me. Especially with what you're paying us. What about you, Marie-Rose?"

She smiled. "I'd like that," she said. "I'd like that very much. As long as Sophie can be here too."

"Of course we must have her as well." The tall man grinned down at Sophie. "So what do you think?"

"Sure thing," Sophie said. And it would get her out of doing dishes every night. She wondered what Mary Ellen would say about her being one of the singers. All of a sudden, she couldn't wait to get to school tomorrow and see her new friend and the other girls. She had such a lot to talk about.

"What about your son, Mrs. LaGrange? He did a great job out there on the ice. We often use local skaters for fill-ins, but he's one of the most talented I've seen. How do you think he'd feel about skating with us for the rest of the week?"

"You could ask him, but I'm quite sure he would be happy to," said Maman.

"Now, I have one more question," Mr. Parfait said, gazing at Auntie Marie-Rose.

She caught her breath. "What's that?"

"I wonder if I could take you out for lunch tomorrow?"

"Oh!" Her eyes widened in surprise. "Oh! Yes, I'd like that. Very much. Thank you."

"Wonderful! I'll pick you up at noon." He raised her hand to his lips and kissed it lingeringly. "Until tomorrow then," he said, and left.

Sophie's mother gathered the rest of her sheet music and Sophie and her aunt followed her out of the organ box.

Henri was waiting for them beside the main entrance. And so were some people wanting to congratulate Maman and Auntie Marie-Rose for the music.

"Just beautiful," one woman was saying.

"Did you reach them?" Sophie whispered to Henri.

He nodded. "They've sent police over to guard all the entrances."

Sophie took in a huge sigh of relief. Her idol, Barbara Ann was going to be safe after all.

Seven people were squashed into the car as Papa drove them home. Henri was going to wait for Joseph and ride with him on the motorcycle later. Sophie was in the backseat wedged between her aunts, and Zephram was sitting on Auntie Marie-Rose's lap.

He patted her damp cheek. "So sad," he said.

She shook her head. "No, Zephie. Not sad at all. It's just those songs. They always make me melancholy."

Auntie Claudine said, "I thought tonight you two sounded

better than the pop singers on the radio. Way better. And Alma, you really outdid yourself with that beautiful organ music."

"Thank you," Maman said. "It's really a very easy organ to play. Nice and new, not like that grouchy old thing at the church I have to battle with every Sunday."

"And our Joseph! Wasn't he great?"

Papa nodded. "He did us proud. You all did."

"What's the story of the skater who left?" Auntie Claudine asked. "What's his name? Ricardo Montaine? Did Barbara Ann say you knew him in high school, Marie-Rose?"

Auntie Marie-Rose nodded. "Yes," she sniffed. "I did."

Auntie Claudine peered at her. "He's not the reason you wanted to come out on this trip, is he? Is he the one that jilted you last month, and went off with some other girl?"

Auntie Marie-Rose nodded again and blotted her eyes with her handkerchief. "I knew him in high school but we met again about a year ago and started going out," she sniffed. "But I'm much better off without him. What a scoundrel he turned out to be! Imagine leaving the whole show and that lovely Mr. Parfait in a lurch like he did. He's so disgusting."

Oh, but he'd looked so wonderful, like a dream, a vision, Sophie was thinking.

"You're right, Marie-Rose." Auntie Claudine leaned over and patted her cousin's knee. "As you say, you're much better off without him. And you know, there are lots more fish in the sea."

"Like that nice Mr. Parfait, maybe?" Sophie asked her.

Auntie Marie-Rose smiled down at her. "You're right, Sophie. Ben Parfait is really sweet, isn't he?"

"Hmm. Maybe I better go along with you two at lunch tomorrow and chaperone," Auntie Claudine said, laughing.

"Oh, you!" Auntie Marie-Rose said. "Don't you dare!" She was smiling, really smiling. That dark shadow in her eyes was vanishing. She was starting to look like her old self. The jolly auntie that Sophie remembered.

Although it was late and the rest of the family had gone to bed, Sophie wasn't asleep yet on the sofa when she heard Joseph's motorcycle grumble to a stop beside the front gate. Two sets of heavy steps clomped up to the porch and into the house. Her brothers were home.

"Joe," she called from the sofa.

He stopped on his way through the living room. Henri went on.

"You're still awake, Soph? You should be asleep by now."

"Did you go back, Joe?" she whispered. "You and Henri?"

"Go where?"

"You know. Back to the gravel pit."

"No. After we heard about the kidnapping scheme, we decided those bikers are all scum. The police said they've been trying to get something on them for months. This gives them a good reason to shut them down and force them to leave town. Besides, I didn't like the way they were treating my little sister."

Sophie grinned at him.

"So Henri and me, we don't want to have anything to do with any of them. Also, after skating the rest of this week in that Hollywood Ice Review show, I'll have to concentrate on getting our hockey team to the provincial finals. Then, who knows, maybe even eventually to the Olympics. For the next few months, hockey's going to take up all my time outside of school. Good thing I've got someone to do all my chores for me."

Sophie groaned.

"A promise is a promise," he reminded her.

"Yeah, yeah, okay," she mumbled.

"Barbara Ann gave me something for you." He pulled an envelope out from inside his jacket and shook out a large photograph.

It was of Barbara Ann standing at the edge of an ice arena, wearing her skating costume and a big smile. "We couldn't have done it without you, Sophie. Thanks a lot," she had written and signed, "Your friend, Barbara Ann Scott, Sept. 9, 1951.

"Wow! Does she know about the, um, kidnapping plot?"

"No, I don't think so. But I heard they're going to double up the security at the arena while they're in town. And at the hotel too. I'm sure the bikers won't try any tricky business now the police are on to them."

Sophie smiled back at the skater's picture. "She's really pretty, isn't she?"

Joseph nodded, staring down at the photo. "Even prettier in real life," he mumbled on his way to the kitchen.

Sophie couldn't wait to show the photograph to her new friends at school tomorrow. Mary Ellen was going to love it. She'll probably want to know all about what it's like to sing at the world famous Hollywood Ice Review.

A light from on top the piano caught Sophie's eye. It was the kitchen light reflecting the sparkles in the tiara on the Barbara Ann Scott doll. Was she winking at Sophie?

Before she could get up and check, Sophie's eyes closed and she was asleep.

"Barbara Ann Scott — the Gretzky of 1948"

"Known as 'Canada's Sweetheart,' Barbara Ann Scott is still the only Canadian to ever win the Olympic Gold Medal at the senior women's figure skating level. Dedication, sheer determination and plain hard work helped her achieve this impressive goal. Her grace, sportsmanship, technical brilliance and modesty, on and off the ice, are remembered more than 50 years later." — Quoted from Library and Archives Canada

- Barbara Ann was born in Ottawa, Ontario, on May 9, 1928, to her proud parents, army Colonel Clyde Rutherford Scott and Mary Purves.

• At age seven, Barbara Ann started skating lessons at Ottawa's Minto Club where she spent many hours perfecting her skills.

• At age ten, Barbara Ann was the youngest Canadian to pass the gold figures test. That year, while visiting her skating hero Sonja Henie in Ottawa, she was given a souvenir autographed photo of Sonja in a gold frame which she treasured for many years.

• When Barbara Ann was eleven, she won the gold medal in the Canadian Junior Figure Skating finals.

• At age thirteen, she became the first female in history to ever land a Double Lutz in competition successfully.

• From 1944 to 1948, Barbara Ann won the Canadian Senior Women's Championship four times and from 1945 to 1948, she won the North American Championships every year.

• When she was eighteen, Barbara Ann won the gold medal for figure skating at the World Championships in Stockholm, Sweden. She was the first North American to do so since it began in 1896.

• On February 6, 1948, Barbara Ann won Canada's first Olympic gold medal in women's figure skating at St. Moritz, Switzerland, at the fifth Winter

Olympic Games. Later that year, she was inducted into Canada's Olympic Hall of Fame.

• In June 1948, she gave up her amateur status to begin her professional career. She skated at the famous Roxy Theatre in New York and from 1949 to 1953, she toured Canada, the USA and England with the Hollywood Ice Review, starring as "Canada's Sweetheart."

• After her Olympic Gold medal win, the Reliable Toy Company created a Barbara Ann Scott doll. It became so enormously popular that for many years different annual versions of the doll were created.

• In 1955, Barbara Ann married Thomas Van Dyke King, whom she met when he was a publicity agent for the Hollywood Ice Review.

• In 1991, Barbara Ann was presented with the Order of Canada for her services to figure skating.

• In 2007, Skate Canada renamed its headquarters in Ottawa, Ontario, in her honour.

• Barbara Ann Scott has remained active in the figure skating world where she serves as a judge at professional competitions. She has also trained and showed horses for which she has won many equestrian medals. She has authored two books about figure skating for children.

• She now lives in Florida with her husband, Thomas King.

During her skating career, Barbara Ann Scott was even more famous than Wayne Gretzky is today. She made our nation proud and she brought grace and elegance to the sport of figure skating. But even more important, she was, and remains, an inspiration to many young people who have a dream of someday achieving Olympic Gold.

About the Author

Norma Charles is the author of many books for children including the Moonbeam Bronze Medal Award winner, *The Girl in the Backseat,* and the Chocolate Lily Award winner, *All the Way to Mexico.* As a young girl she attended school in New Westminster and enjoyed ice skating at Queen's Park Arena, where she was thrilled to see the famous ice skater Barbara Ann Scott skating as Canada's Sweetheart in the Hollywood Ice Review. Norma lives in Vancouver, British Columbia.

Marquis Book Printing Inc.

Québec, Canada
2009